A Broom with a View

Book 1 in the Kentucky Witches

A Broom with a View

Copyright © 2015 by Rebecca Patrick-Howard

www.rebeccaphoward.net

Published by Mistletoe Press

All rights reserved. No part of this book may be reproduced, scanned, or distributed in any printed or electronic form without permission.

First Edition: December 2015

Printed in the United States of America

For Wilma Lewis & Betty Burnam (the real Nana Bud)

Chapter One

LIZA JANE Higginbotham was a witch.

Mind you, not the kind of witch that conversed with black cats or could make herself look like a supermodel with a wave of her hand (although that particular skill would've been useful on a number of occasions) but a witch, nonetheless.

When she was twelve she'd watched a movie about a girl who came into her witchy powers on her sixteenth birthday. "Teen Witch," it was called.

She wasn't *that* kind of witch either.

Liza Jane had been born a witch, known it most of her life, and considered it as normal as her hair color.

(Okay, maybe not *quite* as normal as her hair color. Thanks to Clairol and some plastic gloves, she'd been dying her hair for so long she had no idea what her natural color was.)

Nope, she thought as she gave the last box on the U-Haul a good, solid kick with her tennis shoe and sent it flying down the icy ramp, *she was just a regular witch with few useful and exciting skills.*

Sure, she could get rid of negative energy around a place, was a pretty good healer, and could see into the future with a little bit of help from some of her tools–but she couldn't make herself invisible or turn people into frogs.

Had she been a *TV* kind of witch, she'd have just wrinkled her nose a few times and in an orderly fashion sent those boxes flying into her grandparents' old farm house, where they then would've graciously unpacked themselves. Then she would've spent the rest of the afternoon lounging on a perfectly made bed (*not* made by her, of course), watching Rom-Coms, and feeding herself strawberries.

And later she would've turned Jennifer Miller into a cockroach. Just for the fun of it.

But she could *not* send all the boxes into the house like that, she couldn't afford to get cable, and there were no strawberries available in Kudzu Valley in December.

Shivering even inside her thermal coat, Liza Jane rubbed her chapped hands together and hopped down from the back of the truck. She blew out a puff of air, her breath making a large round cloud before floating away, and watched as the box slid off the ramp and landed with a thud at the bottom. One side was completely caved in. She hoped there wasn't anything breakable in it. She hadn't taken the time to mark any of them. It was going to be complete chaos for awhile.

Divorce was making her more unorganized than usual.

And she was still a little miffed that she'd missed Thanksgiving back north. But she'd had to get out of there as quickly as possible. She'd had to, even if it meant eating chicken nuggets and fries instead of turkey.

"What the *hell* was I thinking?" she muttered to herself as she turned and looked at her new house.

Well, technically, her *old* house. She had lived there, once upon a time. She'd been six then and now she was in her thirties so it had been...

Well, she didn't need to think about how many years ago that was. She was already depressed enough as it was.

Her grandparents' white farm house rose before her in the dreary winter sky, proud and neglected. White paint had chipped off and now sprinkled the dead, brown grass like dirty snow, leaving behind naked patches of worn wood. An upstairs window was boarded up, the glass missing. A black garbage bag covered another. A window unit in the second floor master bedroom had leaked and dripped over the years, leaving a stream of discolored water running down the side of the house. She was almost certain the front porch was leaning, too.

Liza Jane cocked her head to one side and studied it. *Yep, she thought, it was definitely crooked.*

"At least it has electricity and running water," she stated cheerfully.

Nothing answered her back. She was surrounded by more than fifty acres of mountainside and pastureland. Her grandparents' farm. Her *family* farm. Her heritage.

Damn, it was dismal.

She knew it would look better in the summertime, when the trees were bursting and full of leaves and color, the fields were lush with wildflowers and thick grass, and the sky a brilliant blue.

But for now everything was dead. Dead and gray. Even the tree branches were gray. How was that *possible*?

Her divorce was almost final. She just needed to sign the papers. Her high school sweetheart had left her for the woman at Starbucks who made him his latte every morning. (Well, actually he was marrying the trombone player in the pop opera group he managed. He'd just initially left her for the Starbucks chick. There had, apparently, been many women. Many, *many* women.)

Back in Boston she'd lost her fairly interesting and well-paying job as the administrative assistant to the director at the nonprofit organization she'd been with for two years. She'd been unceremoniously fired when everyone on her floor, including some donors, overheard her yelling obscenities over the phone to her husband's lawyer.

She'd let the happy new couple have her house in Wakefield. She'd loved that house, had enjoyed everything about it. But once she'd discovered that Latte-Girl had gotten busy on her kitchen table and Trombone Chick had blown more than her mouthpiece on Liza Jane's $2,000 leather sofa, the bloom kind of fell off the rose.

"You're being very immature about this," her husband, Mode, had told her when she'd handed him her house key.

In her mind, Liza had stuck her tongue out at him and snarked, *I thought you thought people overused the word "very."* Instead, she'd kept her face impassive.

"You own this house outright," he'd continued, growing increasingly agitated by her lack of fight. "You don't have a *job*.

You won't be able to support yourself. Your money will run out soon. You've *never* been good at money management, Liza. It makes no sense for you to leave the house. Jennifer and I will be fine someplace else. We won't have any problems settling in." He'd paused at that moment and leaned in closer to her. Then, with their faces only inches apart, he'd put his hand on her arm. "It's *you* I'm worried about."

His self-righteousness had been the last straw. She'd told him where he could stick her house key.

Now, since she'd signed over the house to him and he'd given her half its appraised worth, she was moving back into the only other thing she owned besides her ratty car–her grandparents' dilapidated farm house in Kudzu Valley, Kentucky.

Liza Jane was depressed.

"Promise me you won't kill yourself," her mother, Mabel, had shrilled over the phone on Liza's drive down. "Nobody would even know forever, you being out there by yourself like that!"

"Please consider medication or a therapist," Mode had cajoled her with fake worry and sincerity.

"Don't do anything stupid down there," her younger sister, Bryar Rose, had warned her. "Like join Scientology or get bangs."

"Well, maybe just a *little* something," she muttered, flipping her hair back from her face, her teeth chattering in the gusty wind.

For a moment, the air around her stilled. The time-honored words she chanted ascended from her like a soft breeze, comforting her with their familiarity and cadence. They gently lifted the ends of her hair and swept across her face like motherly hands, their warmth nearly bringing tears to her eyes. Her heart raced and for just a second she felt a surge of adrenalin, like she could take on the world if she wanted.

And then it stopped.

Grinning with satisfaction, Liza opened her eyes and studied the farm house again. The porch was perfectly straight, not a board out of place.

"Yeah, well, I deserved it," she snapped to the crows that flew overhead.

Then, feeling a little drained and hung over from what she'd just done, Liza Jane proudly marched up her new steps and into her new life.

***

When Liza Jane had last been in Kudzu Valley it had boasted a Taco Bell, Burger King, and McDonalds. There was talk back then of putting in a Walmart on the new by-pass that circled around the mountain and circumvented the small downtown area that consisted of two cross streets and one red light.

That Walmart never materialized; the by-pass was a lonesome stretch of road that passed through what used to be farm land and a drive-in. Five families had lost land to it all in the name of progress. It did, however, get travelers to the next county over three minutes faster. This was important since Morel County was dry, making it impossible to (legally) buy any kind of alcohol.

Liza's grandfather, Paine, had died ten years earlier. Her grandmother, Nana Bud, had passed away two years ago. The old farm house had been empty ever since, although it had been winterized and a neighbor had watched over it and taken care of any repairs it needed.

Liza had gone down and taken a look at things back in the summer, before her big move, so she kind of knew what she was getting herself into. Still, there weren't many conveniences. For one thing, it was completely devoid of food, unless you wanted to count the bag of birdseed that someone (her grandfather probably) had left out on the back porch in the 1980s and the small piece of moldy cheese that had led a mouse to his last fatal adventure.

Liza Jane needed supplies.

Other than the tiny food marts attached to some of the gas stations, there was only one grocery store in the entire county. It was a discount chain that sold fatty beef, bait, generic canned food, and bulk bags of cheap cereal.

She could roll with that. At least it was cheap. And right now she needed cheap. She was not only moving to Kudzu Valley, she was opening her own business. The money her grandmother had left her two years ago and the divorce settlement would not last forever.

She'd declined alimony.

As Liza slowly pushed her cart down the unfamiliar aisles and loaded up with boxes of Rice Crisps and Frosty Tiny Wheats, Liza became acutely aware of someone's eyes drilling holes into her.

Her senses stayed at a heightened state of awareness these days; when she'd let them slide in the past her husband had gone on a one-man tour of the local single ladies and she wasn't going to make *that* mistake again. However, she did make an effort to turn her senses down when she was out in public so that she didn't pick up on every Dick, Jane, and Bubba's feelings and thoughts but even a Normal would've felt the sharp eyes stabbing into their back.

"Liza Jane Merriweather!" The loud, reedy shrill came from less than ten feet behind her and had Liza startled, despite her mindfulness.

When she turned, Liza was face to face with a tiny, elderly woman carrying a yellow shopping basket overflowing with at least two dozen packages of frozen spinach. Unlike many of the other shoppers, who looked like they'd stumbled out of bed without getting dressed or brushing their hair or teeth, the little woman before her wore a blue-tailored suit and was in full makeup.

Her lavender eyeshadow framed small, beady eyes behind thick bifocals and her clunky heels sounded like shotgun blasts as she marched over to where Liza Jane patiently waited. Her hair, permed and sprayed within an inch of its life, was a brilliant purple.

Liza closed her eyes for a moment and reached forward, focusing on the woman's mind. She frantically attempted to extract a name or memory, since it was obvious she was meant to know the person whose arms were now outstretched and gearing up for a hug.

The only word she could come up with was "Pebbles."

"Just look at *you!*" the woman crooned, squeezing Liza Jane in a bony, yet tight, embrace. The combination of Marlboro

Lights, Aqua Net, and Elizabeth Taylor's White Diamonds was almost overpowering. "You're so grown up now!"

Liza plastered what she hoped was a respectful smile across her face and gently untangled herself. She was afraid to squeeze back too hard; in spite of the woman's grip her shoulders and arms felt brittle. God forbid she break somebody on her first day out in town.

"Yes," she replied courteously. "I've grown up a little."

"Liza Jane Merriweather," the woman murmured again, shaking her head in apparent disbelief. Her hair didn't move an inch. Liza had to restrain herself from reaching out and touching it. "I just *can't* believe it."

"Well, actually it's Higginbotham now," Liza helpfully corrected her. "I got married."

"Oh?" At the mention of a husband the woman's eyes sparkled. "Is he here with you?" She began looking around, as though Liza might have hidden him under a gallon of milk in her shopping cart.

"Er..." Liza felt her face turning red. "He's um, back in Boston. We're still, uh, getting some things together. For the move down here."

There was no need to go into the messy details of her impending divorce right there in the grocery store aisle. People were already stopping, pretending to be keenly interested in the nutritional values on the backs of discount cereal boxes while they listened to the two women chat.

"Oh, well, that's okay. I bet you don't remember my name. Do you remember my name," she demanded.

Liza, taken off guard, found herself flustered as she regarded the impatient woman. She reached out again, but came back with nothing. If she'd known her in the past, it was as a child and she'd made little to no impression on Liza.

"Well, I er, I *think* so..." Liza murmured, embarrassed. *Give me a break, lady, it's been almost thirty years*, she thought to herself at the same time.

"It's *Penny*! Penny Libbels!" she cried, slapping Liza Jane on the arm with unexpected strength. "I was your granny's best friend, may she rest in peace."

"Oh, *Pebbles*," Liza Jane nodded now. "Okay, that makes more sense."

"You never *could* say my name right." Penny stared at her wide-eyed and Liza wondered if she was waiting for her to try to say it *now*.

"Um, well, I was young I guess," Liza faltered.

Liza had never been particularly good at small talk. Or grocery stores.

"I hear that you're opening one of those New Agey herbal shops here," Penny pressed, squinting her purple eyes under the harsh fluorescent lights. "You aren't gonna be selling those *drugs* are you? That *meth*?"

At least three more people stopped what they were doing and turned to look back at them, not even trying to hide their curiosity. Liza randomly grabbed at a can of pineapples behind her and clutched it tightly, its metal hard and reassuring under her fingertips. She was about to dig a hole into her hands from the wringing and had already popped an acrylic.

"Well, um, no," she sputtered. "Nothing illegal. It's a holistic clinic, a day spa really, with herbal remedies and massages and–"

"Not one of those places with *hookers*," Penny lowered her voice to a stage whisper, her eyes darting around as she pursed her lips.

"Oh no! Just teas and lotions and regular old massages. Nothing bad," Liza promised.

Oh dear Lord, make me disappear, she prayed silently.

Liza thought she might pass out. One woman passing by actually grabbed her young son by the arm and pushed him ahead of her, as though Liza was already a lady of the night, hawking her body and illegal drugs in the fruit and cereal aisle.

"Hmmm," Penny pursed her lips again so tightly they were almost white. "Well, you *might* do okay here. We're not Hollywood, though. I don't know how many people need those

New Agey things. We got a," her voice dropped back down to a stage whisper, "*chiropractor* last year."

Liza nodded her head, pretending to understand the implication.

"He's just *now* starting to catch on," Penny continued. "The ladies here are good Christian women and they don't like being touched in certain places by men who aren't their husbands. But I suppose since you're a woman, it will be just fine."

Penny did not look hopeful.

It was now all Liza Jane could do to keep a straight face. The can of pineapples began to shake in her unsteady hands as she forced her body to control itself. She mentally gathered her thoughts together and forced her breathing to slow down and ease up. Then she ran a quick, but effective, little charm through her mind that sent a wave of coolness through her body, relaxing her muscles and nerves. It wasn't much, but it would hold until she reached the check-out counter.

"Well, I certainly hope people will give me a chance," Liza replied diplomatically once she'd collected herself together.

"Well, at least you don't *have* to work since your husband has a good job. Rosebud was always bragging about his work with the music group. I'm sure your little business will get along just fine and dandy. It's nice for a lady to have a hobby these days," Penny crooned, patting Liza Jane on the arm. "I'd better skedaddle now. I'm making a pot roast for dinner after church tomorrow. Have you found a church yet?"

"I, er..."

"Never mind. You're coming to mine! Elk Creek Primitive. We don't allow none of that singing or music nonsense that the Baptists and Methodists seem to carry on about but you'll *love* our services. They run all morning and our preacher truly gets the spirit deep inside him. I will see you at ten!"

Before Liza could answer, Penny was scurrying off through the considerable number of onlookers, her purple hair a helmet raging her into battle towards the produce.

Since it was a dry county and beer was unavailable, Liza turned and headed back to the candy aisle.

She was going to need a lot more chocolate than she'd initially planned for.

***

In spite of the old house's "quirks" ("quirks" sounded less intimidating than "problems") she loved it. It was spacious and full of charm and character.

More importantly, it smelled and *felt* like her grandparents, and she missed them something fierce. She hadn't visited them nearly as much as she'd wanted to as a child, and hardly at all as an adult. Still, they had regularly gone north and visited Liza, her mother, and her sister on the major holidays and during Paine's vacations.

Liza had looked forward to their visits more than she'd looked forward to the holidays themselves.

Liza didn't think there was a finer woman in the world than her Nana Bud had been, and most everyone who'd known Rosebud in her lifetime would have probably agreed.

Liza's heart had broken when Rosebud passed away.

Her death was especially difficult for Liza since she'd been in Spain with her husband at the time and, due to the standard form of miscommunication exhibited by her mother and Bryar Rose, she hadn't found out about it until her grandmother was already dead and in the ground.

Liza, filled with grief she didn't know she was capable of feeling (she didn't remember her father *or* his death) she'd lashed out at everyone from her husband to the poor plumber who'd just come to the house to unclog the guest toilet. In fact, her relationship with her sister Bryar was still strained and had only started to improve when talk of her divorce from Mode began.

Nothing brought sisters, or women in general, together more than a shared enemy, and Bryar always *had* enjoyed being in the middle of drama.

Liza regretted not attending the funeral; she was even more ashamed that she hadn't seen her grandmother in more than a year when she died. She'd always assumed there would be more time.

She guessed everyone thought that.

Liza Jane thought the guilt of not being there for someone who loved you and having nobody to blame but yourself had to be one of the most dreadful feelings in the world. It was for her, anyway. Rather than being at her grandmother's side, she'd been following her husband around like a puppy on the beaches of Marbella during breaks while he gawked at the topless women and their rosy nipples.

She'd been there when her grandfather Paine had passed away peacefully at the Hospice Center. She'd even been holding his hand when it happened. But that was different.

She'd loved her grandfather but hadn't known him well. He'd always been a quiet, gentle soul who didn't offer much of himself to anyone but his wife. And he'd lived a good, long life. When he'd passed on, Liza had been sad but it had felt *right*. He'd suffered for so long, his death was as much as a relief as it was a release.

As soon as they're returned from England, the last leg of the tour, Liza had locked herself in the guest room. It was the only place in the house Mode said he felt comfortable with her keeping her "supplies" as he called them. (He'd always claimed he was fine with her being a witch and had even considered it a fun little novelty at first, but now Liza was convinced that he'd been partly afraid of her. And rightly so. He *should* have been afraid. Very afraid.)

She'd stayed in that room for two days, holding her own vigil for Nana Bud. On her altar, she'd lit candles and placed Rosebud's picture and some of the cards she'd sent Liza over the years. She'd chanted, she'd meditated, and she'd offered thanks for having someone like her in her life. She'd called to the elements and sought peace within herself.

Mostly, she grieved.

Mode had left her alone. When she'd emerged at the end of the second day, hungry and exhausted, he'd glanced up from a

Science Fiction book he was reading and asked her what she wanted for supper, like she'd just returned home from the movies.

"Jerkwad," Liza muttered now as she remembered the moment in total clarity.

Not all witches were made alike. While they could do similar things and for similar reasons, they were all individuals and had their own unique traits. Unfortunately, sometimes for Liza, one of her strongest traits was that she could remember things that happened ten years ago in total, accurate detail as though they'd occurred just moments earlier. She wished that gift had kicked in while her father was still alive but, like some of the other things she'd learned about herself, witchery and the skills it entailed seemed to be an ongoing process.

But as for Mode..."*Jerkwad*" was one of the nicest things she'd called him. When *his* grandmother had died, she'd been there for him. She'd even arranged the funeral, since both of Mode's parents were dead.

And she'd taken care of all the guests who had filed in and out of the house after the internment. He, on the other hand, never brought up *her* grandmother again. Didn't even offer to send flowers to the cemetery.

Asshat.

Now, as she paced alone through the rooms of the old farm house and touched its walls, feeling the same places her grandparents had also touched, she could feel a part of them near her. It was both peaceful and comforting, even when thoughts of Mode threatened to tear her up inside. (Asshat or Jerkwad aside, they *had* been married for a long time and she *was* grieving a part of him–the part she wanted him to be anyway.)

The overstuffed chairs covered in rainbow-colored afghans held imprints from their bottoms. The stale scent of cigarette smoke (even after being diagnosed with lung cancer her Papaw Paine hadn't given up his Marlboros) that still lingered in the air even after eight years, lace doilies on every flat surface, hundreds of ceramic teapots and ladybug statues, and homemade rag rugs scattered throughout the house were constant reminders of the two people who'd meant the world to her.

Liza vaguely remembered living there in the house with her mother and sister after her father died but those memories felt more like dreams. Still, while they might not have been strong, something about the house *felt* like home anyway. When she'd returned to Kudzu Valley to take stock of the situation after her separation from Mode, she'd known instantly that the idea she was flirting with in her mind was the right one.

As soon as she'd turned off the main road and entered the downtown proper, a calmness had settled over her. The mountains were lush with leaves then, their colors almost unnatural. She'd rolled down her windows and deeply inhaled the town right there on Main Street.

The air itself tasted of freedom.

And when the old farm house had come into view, despite the headache she was getting from the various washouts in the gravel, she'd *felt* her name being called.

Liza had no experience when it came to living in the country, or even living in a small town—at least no recent experience.

"You lived at home for college for Chrissakes!" her mother had scolded her. "You've never even been responsible for a house by yourself!"

Which was true, unless you wanted to consider the fact that Mode only did what he thought he *had* to.

"You've never lived more than a ten-minute walk to a store," her sister had pointed out, which was *also* true, although to Bryar "the Boondocks" meant someplace that couldn't get Chinese delivered to you thirty minutes or less.

At least in her adult life, Liza had *never* lived in isolation, never lived without neighbors within a stone's throw distance, never lived without an active nightlife and restaurant scene just minutes away (now, if she wanted to go to a nightclub, she'd have to drive for more than an hour and a half), and had never been responsible for only herself.

Hell, she'd only even lived by herself just recently. After moving out she'd ended up renting a dinky little apartment in Beverly that cost a fortune but had a closet the size of a shoebox and a view of a couple who were either newlyweds or just really, really amorous.

Still, standing there in the yard, *her* yard now, and feeling the ground beneath her feet–the same ground generations of her relatives had stood on as well, she knew she was home.

She knew it as a witch; she knew it as a woman.

"You can *have* it," Bryar Rose had sworn as soon as Liza asked her permission to move into it. "What the hell am I going to do with it?"

Her mother had echoed the sentiment.

She didn't remember the shotgun house on Ann Street where she'd lived with her real father or the trips to the local park she'd apparently taken with him when he was alive (though she'd seen the pictures). Her only memories of Kudzu Valley had come from her brief and infrequent visits growing up. In her college sociology class, however, she'd read about how people from Appalachia could get the mountains in their blood and never really shake them. No matter where they went, the mountains stayed with them, softly beckoning them to return home.

Liza figured she was one of those people. All those years of living in the city, she'd teared up every time she'd watched "Matewan" or "Coal Miner's Daughter" or even "Next of Kin" and "Justified." Movies set in eastern Kentucky or nearby had pulled at her, even the bad ones, and she'd watched the credits feeling a yearning, like she was missing something she'd never even had.

***

The farm house had four bedrooms and two had actual bedroom furniture. Another was what looked like her grandmother had used for a junk room. It was a mess but, more importantly, if she was going to get that board off the window and replace the glass she'd have to straighten it up. As it was, there was no direct path to get to the other side of the room.

There wasn't a *path* at all.

The room was full of boxes of patterns dating back to the 1970s, scraps of random material, Christmas tree lights, bags of unopened junk mail, and boxes of 3-ply toilet paper. Seriously, there was more toilet paper than two people could ever use. And her grandfather had been gone for a long time.

"Aw Nana Bud," Liza chuckled. "You really got the use out of your Sam's Club membership, didn't you?"

Well, at least she wouldn't have to stock up on that necessity any time soon. Nana Bud had always believed in being prepared; you could never have too much toilet paper or chicken broth.

She bought both every time she left the house, even if it was to just make a run to the post office.

With Luke Bryan blaring on the portable CD player she'd found in the room she was using as her own bedroom, Liza sashayed around, singing along and bobbing her head in time with the music while she sorted and organized.

She'd listened to country music stations on the whole ride down. It might have sounded stupid to others, but one of the things that excited her about living in Kudzu Valley was the thought of being a part of those things the songs talked about: a sense of community, bonfires with neighbors, and adventurous drives down backroads that turned to dirt...

After what she'd been through with Mode and his menagerie of extracurricular activities, she couldn't wait to dive into the bucolic life those singers crooned about and live a more peaceful existence.

Goodbye to pop opera bands, naked boobs on the beach, and 2:00 am Chinese. Hello to four wheeling (whatever that *really* was), horseback riding (she could learn), and gardening (she *did* have a green thumb).

When Luke got into his song about the woman dancing in his truck, Liza, who was in the middle of bending over to pick up an old tennis racket, paused mid-air.

Did she need a truck?

Oh, she thought with glee. *Maybe I **do** need a truck.*

The idea thrilled her to the bone–the thought of cruising through town sitting high above the road, being able to haul...stuff.

But she changed her mind as quickly as the idea came to her. She *had* a car and Christabel had been good to her. More than that, when she made the payment on her next week, she'd own her free and clear.

And it only took six years.

"Okay, okay," she grumbled aloud, just in case Christabel had been able to hear her thoughts and desires from her position in the driveway. There were times when Liza was certain her car had a sixth sense, but she hadn't been able to prove it yet. "No truck for me. I have a good car."

Sighing with regret, Liza leaned back over to reach for the tennis racket again and then popped back up.

"Hey," she cried, her eyes bright with excitement. "Do I need a *gun*?!"

A heavy box of books fell off the top of a shelf just then and came within a hair of crashing down on her toes. Liza had reacted quickly enough that she was able to stop it mid-air and gently move it a few feet to the left before letting it continue its drop.

"Yeah, yeah, yeah," she muttered again. "I hear you. Grandpa. Or Nana. Or whichever one of my dead relatives you might be. I won't get a gun. I don't even know how to use one."

Before returning to work Liza did stop and listen to the room for a few minutes, however. If there *had* been another energy there moments ago, it was gone now.

If either one of her grandparents had been watching over her, and in the very room with her, they were no longer there.

Liza was sorry about that.

Chapter Two

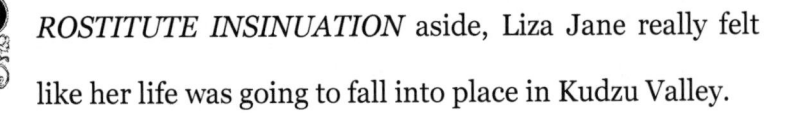

PROSTITUTE INSINUATION aside, Liza Jane really felt like her life was going to fall into place in Kudzu Valley.

Her new business, The Healing Hands, was on the corner of Main Street and Broadway. At one time Kudzu Valley was a thriving railroad town, a town built to house the workers of the tracks that ran right through the middle of downtown. The houses and businesses were all laid out in a perfect grid, a perfectly planned community.

At one time the town boasted not one but *two* cinemas, a handful of restaurants, two department stores, and several dozen locally-owned businesses.

There had even been a drive-in and Liza could almost remember going to it as a child, sitting on the hood of the car with nachos and popcorn between her and a man who was now blurry in her mind.

However, things had changed. More of the storefronts were empty than used now, their dusty windows overlooking a street that saw little traffic. Liza expected to see a tumbleweed blow by at any moment.

A crazy part of her considered running out in the middle of the road and laying down under the one and only red light, just to see how long it took for a car to come by.

But that would've been immature. Right?

Now everyone just drove to the next county over; the next county that served alcohol and had a Walmart.

Still, whether the town was dead or not it still needed *her* kind of business; she was sure of it. There wasn't a single place in town where anyone could get a massage and more and more people were looking for natural treatments for their ailments. There were forty-thousand people in Morel County and some of them were bound to get sick and in need of somebody to pound on their backs and legs for half an hour.

Liza Jane Higginbotham was just the person to do the pounding. She had a lot of issues to work out.

It took her several tries to get the key to turn in the lock. When kicking, cursing, and throwing a mini tantrum with her red hair flying from her knitted cap and whipping her in the face didn't work, she turned to something else.

Liza calmed down, gave up the lock and key, said a quiet little charm to herself, and then let go of the knob and watched as the door creaked open in reluctant welcome.

"Yeah, well, you and I need to work on that," she murmured as she stepped inside.

Of course, she wouldn't *always* be able to charm it open. She'd have to figure out what made it stick and get that fixed and go about things the right way as often as she could. In the meantime, however, she was keen to explore her new building now and she didn't want to wait.

There were three rooms downstairs: a large space upfront, a bathroom, and a smaller room in the back.

The smaller room was around 10 x 20, an awkward size, and had unfortunate peeling linoleum on the floor (and smelled faintly of pickles for no discernible reason whatsoever) but she could work with it. With new floors, new paint on the walls, a privacy screen where people could change clothes, and some aromatherapy it would be a fine treatment room.

Someone had tried painting the bathroom a shocking shade of blood red, without priming it first. The original blue bled through in parts, making it look like someone really *had* splashed blood against the walls. She wasn't totally against the *Texas Chainsaw Massacre* look but figured it might not be soothing to some of her more sensitive clients.

There was also an upstairs' apartment which was available for her use as well. It consisted of a living area with a dining space in the back, a bedroom, a galley kitchen, and a bathroom that had a toilet and shower, but no sink. (The sink wasn't missing; there just wasn't enough room for one.)

Liza had no reason to live in the apartment but she *could* use it for storage. She hoped that her actual products, as well as her services, would bring her some income. She had oils, herbs, tinctures, supplies for making one's *own* tincture, and even gemstones for sale. She'd also ordered a ton of lotions, bubble baths, creams, and organic juices and supplements. She was eager to start making her own body scrubs and shampoos, too, and stock them as well.

She used to get a kick out of making them and using what she could, giving the rest out to friends for Christmas but Mode had ridiculed her for doing it whenever he saw the opportunity.

"Why do you want to keep buying brown sugar and olive oil?" he'd ask with that condescending smirk of his. "I'm making good money now. Just go to the mall and pick out what you want. It will save you a lot of time and you're not really saving us money by doing this. I don't know why you want to do it."

What she *wanted* was to make her own damn bubble bath. She didn't care that the DIY approach wasn't saving them money, she just enjoyed it. And she secretly thought they were safer and better for her skin.

Besides, it wasn't like she had much of anything else to do anymore anyway.

She hadn't worked in years. When she'd gone back to school and received her massage therapist license she'd had a ball doing the certification and being in a classroom setting again. Liza had always liked school. Then she'd taken the job at the day spa and that had been fun, too, even though it was only part time. At least she was getting out of the house.

And her clients *liked* her.

Since she'd married Mode, most of the people she knew were *his* people. There were the bandmates, *their* girlfriends, their publicity people, their accountants, the groupies (oh God, the groupies-who would've thought a pop opera group brought groupies), and so on and so on.

She hadn't had her own "people" in a very, very long time. But then he'd talked her out of working at the day spa, convincing her that she'd be much happier traveling and going on the road with him. "Just think of how much fun we'll have going to South America, Scotland—Japan even! You can do whatever you want while I'm on the road!"

Starry-eyed and full of wanderlust those things *had* sounded great to her at the time. So, even though she'd paid good money to get her license, and she liked the people she worked with, she'd quit her job and let the license expire to become a stay-at-home wife who traveled with her husband.

Of course, in reality the traveling rarely happened. Sure, they'd gone on a few trips at first, and they'd had a wonderful time during those trips. Mode was a different person away from home. He was charming, knowledgeable, and relaxed. The tours were exciting. Those trips had reminded her of why she'd fallen in love with him in the first place.

But later when it came time for him to travel to San Francisco for a week he'd told her that the other members of the group were starting to complain since they couldn't bring *their* spouses with them.

"Sorry honey, but you might want to sit this one out," he'd said with concern.

"But we pay for my way, and my meals. Couldn't their spouses and girlfriends do the same? It's not like the group is paying for me to go."

He'd nodded in agreement and swore a little to show his "irritation." Then he'd said, "Let 'em simmer down a bit. Then you can come on the next one.

Of course, the next one would come around and he'd said the same thing.

"I think I'm going to get my massage license back," she'd declared one June morning, five years ago. "I've painted every single wall in the house, learned to crochet and made more afghans than I ever thought possible, and have dug around in the garden so much I'm afraid if I go any farther I might hit Hell. I need a *life*."

"I like having you at home, though," he'd all but pleaded. "You don't know how much it means to be able to come home to a place that's clean and ready for me. To know someone is inside and has food waiting. The traveling is getting old. You being there for me at home is what makes it bearable."

Liza had gathered her nerves at that point and said what had been on her mind for months. "Well maybe if I got pregnant...I mean, I think we *can* now. And I'm really, really ready."

He'd looked away then, his face blank. When he'd turned back to her he'd been all smiles again. "Well, it might be hard if you're on the road. We're leaving for Bermuda next weekend and you can go with us. I was going to surprise you!"

So, for the next five tours she was "allowed" to travel with them. That had continued on for a year and a half. Then it stopped again. She'd brought up pregnancy three times after that but he'd always changed the subject. She'd finally just stopped.

In hindsight she realized that only *one* of the members had complained of her presence–the one he was currently engaged to.

A trombone player. She'd been too blind to see it, or else too scared to look into it properly.

"Serves me right," she spat.

Her voice, stronger than she'd realized, echoed in the cavernous room. It was a little thrilling. "I spent all my free time helping others see their future. I was too dim-witted to look at my *own* present."

At least she had some money. Along with the house and property, when Nana Bud died she'd left both Liza and Bryar a tidy sum from her life insurance policy and stocks she'd purchased back in the 1970s. In total, Liza Jane's part came to more than $125,000. (Which made her wonder what her grandmother had left Mabel. She'd never asked her mother.)

At one time, it would've been a fortune. Now she was going to have to make it stretch a good while to cover her expenses for at least two years, until her own business hopefully (definitely, think *positive*) took off.

So far she'd used it to rent the apartment in Beverly, move to Kentucky, get the house up and running, pay the rent for her building four months in advance, purchase all the supplies she needed to get her business up and running (massage table, products, waiting room furniture, decorations, etc.), her recertification, and to get the utilities on for everything.

And then there had been a few new outfits. Just because.

She shuddered at the amount she'd already spent.

"I *will* make this happen," she promised herself, tossing her head back so that her hair shook in the shadowy light. "This *is* going to work for me."

The overhead lights flickered off and on, a strobe-light effect from the energy that flew from the snap of her fingers.

She felt good, she felt positive.

She was going to do this, do this well, and not use any magic at all.

Oh, who was she kidding? She'd use as much as she could. A girl *had* to eat, after all.

***

Liza knew whose voice she'd hear on the other end of the line before she was halfway across the room. Always a glutton for punishment, she continued towards the phone all the same. It was either now or later, after all.

Mode's voice carried that pleasant, cheery tone that had irritated her so much at the end and made her swoon in the beginning.

"Hi Mode," she said carefully, and then cringed. She'd promised herself to avoid that if she could.

Nana Bud had believed that names had a tremendous amount of power attached to them, some of the greatest power that existed.

"Don't use someone's name when you're mad or flying off the handle," she'd warned her when Liza was nine and first starting to recognize the fact that she could do things that others couldn't. "If you use their name in anger, you're trapping both of you in a web you'll likely never get out of. And the same—don't say it in love unless you're real sure you mean it. That's the thing that will bind you best of all."

Still, as she spoke Mode's name aloud she was reminded of the number of times her mother had made fun of it.

"*Mode*," she'd shuddered. "That's ridiculous. It sounds too much like '*commode*.' He should at least go by a nickname. He shouldn't tempt the fates like that."

"I'm assuming you're settling in down there in little old Kudzu," he said.

Condescending prick, she said soundlessly and then watched as the book she'd left on the coffee table the night before shot up in the air and slammed back down, sending the TV remote clattering to the floor.

She was really going to have to get a grip on her emotions. Now was as good a time as any to start trying.

And maybe she should give him the benefit of the doubt. After all, her goal was to live a peaceful life that was free of stress and unwanted excitement. She could start by being civil. Besides, she couldn't be sure if he was *truly* being condescending or if it was his legitimate attempt at being cute/friendly and just sounded smarmy because she was currently pissed off at him for cheating on her and ending their marriage.

Oh, screw peaceful and relaxing, her inner mind snapped. There'd be plenty of time for that later. She'd stick with the condescension because that's just the kind of mood Mode put her in anymore.

So far in the conversation, he'd rambled on about himself for at least six minutes, giving her information about his upcoming tour and problems with the guest bathroom's pipes in her old, *their* old house.

"Lizey?" he asked, his chipper tone falling an octave. "I asked if you were settling in down there."

"Fine and dandy," she replied tightly. "I'm assuming *you're* settling into little old Jennifer."

"Jennifer's fine," he replied, not losing the smile from his voice but speaking slowly, as though speaking to an insolent child.

"Are you sure you're holding up? It's an awfully big house for just one person and you're not used to being by yourself and having to do things alone."

Except for all those weeks you went off and left me alone while you were on tour, she mentally snapped back at him. "I'm fine," she replied instead. "I like being by myself. At least I know I am in good company."

"But still...you know you can always come back up here when you're ready. Your mom or sister will be sure to take you in and help you."

Every hair on Liza's head rose to angry attention. *You don't even know who I am*, she wanted to scream at the top of her lungs. *You never let me be myself so you don't know what I am capable of! Don't you remember? Don't you remember that first year and what...?*

Her silence appeared to make him nervous. "Is there anything I can do for you on my end? Any way I can help you with, you know, official business?"

What he *really* wanted to know was if he could do anything to help her clear the rest of her part of their storage unit out faster. If he could do anything to stop the loose ends of mail she figured were still being delivered to his house. If there was anything he could do to speed up the divorce process...

He was asking if he could do anything to help cut their ties to each other quicker.

"Not a darn thing," she said. "I'm moving just as fast as I can."

"Oh! I know you are! I didn't mean to imply that you were dragging your heels or anything," he said smoothly.

Yeah, the way you didn't drag your heels when you invited your mistress to move in with you before I'd even packed my suitcase, she thought wryly.

"Now we'll be out of town for all of next month," he said. "I'm going on tour with the group and we have sixteen dates on the west coast. So if there's anything you need from up here—"

"You telling me so that I can come up then and you two won't have to run into me?" she finished for him. "Because I can tell you now that I won't be coming up there until after Christmas, probably. I have to start working on my business this week. I have men coming in next week to start construction and I can't leave them alone without any supervision."

Liza, who'd sat through most of the conversation feeling a bit depressed, straightened her back now, proud at how official she'd sounded. *Ha! Take that. I have work, too!*

"No! That's not what I meant at all. I just meant that Larry and Sheila next door have the spare key," he replied, his voice beginning to sound a little strained.

Liza was now confused. Her mind began to spin as she traveled backwards in time to the incident involving the house key and the ensuing argument. "Well, I still have my key. Remember? I tried to return it to you and you wouldn't accept it. You brought it to my apartment and said that I needed to keep it until everything was final, until the house was completely in your name."

"Yes, well, we um..." Mode let his voice trail off his until his end of the line fell uncomfortably silent. It was in the silence that the implication of what he was saying struck Liza square in the middle of the forehead.

Damn her third eye.

"You had the locks changed," she accused him, unable to keep the high pitch of anger from creeping into her voice. "Well I'll be damned."

Mode coughed nervously and through the line she could see the tips of his ears, rosy from the anxiety he was feeling. Soon he'd be unbuttoning the top of his shirt. *Good.* "It's just that there's been a lot of thefts in the neighborhood recently and–"

Enjoying his discomfort more than any decent person should, Liza allowed him to ramble while she closed her eyes and let herself drift hundreds of miles away and back in time.

On the movie screen behind her eyelids she could see them a few days ago, the catalyst for the current conversation.

There was Mode, with his stubby beard, tweed jacket he'd picked up at Goodwill, and red suspenders that she'd always thought looked ridiculous but kept quiet about because she didn't want to hurt his feelings.

And then there was Jennifer, pacing around the living room like a caged cat in her black tights and deep orange tunic sweeping her knees. Her voice was controlled but her skinny little shoulders were hunched forward and her eyes were bright with blue-tinted rage. "I don't want that *woman* to have a key to my house Mode."

"She's not 'that woman' Jen. Liza's a great girl. She'd never do anything to hurt you or us!" Mode, who abhorred conflict, looked crushed. His eyes were lowered to the travertine tile Eliza had installed two years earlier and his mouth dropped at the corners—the way it got when he thought the world was stacked against him.

"She's vindictive and mean-spirited and I don't trust her as far as I can throw her," Jennifer spat. "Change the locks!"

Liza chuckled at the scene playing out before her eyes on her own private movie screen.

She was the vindictive one who couldn't be trusted? She hadn't been the one to make it her goal to sleep with a married man on a twelve-city tour and document the affair in Instagram posts.

Liza still couldn't believe they'd carried on that affair as long as they had without her knowing. When he'd told her about the Starbucks girl and that he was moving out, she'd thought he'd gone insane. Insanity she could fix. But when she learned he was actually leaving her for someone he worked with, that was different. That was serious. That's when she knew she'd lost him.

Mode was still babbling some nonsense when she interrupted him. "Sorry, I've got something on the stove. I'd better go."

"What? You're cooking! That's great. I am so glad that you're—"

She'd never know which part of her cooking made him "glad" because she hung up before he finished.

Eh well, she shrugged as she stared at the blue light on her phone's screen.

Perhaps she *was* a little vindictive. After all, she hadn't made an entirely innocent exit from their house. With Bryar at her side, begging Liza to let her curse something or put out a good hex, she'd loosened some things in all the toilets so that they'd overflow and run for the entire two weeks that the happy couple was on vacation, removed the new thermostat which effectively left them without air or heat until they could call someone in to replace it, and then removed all the towel racks and light bulbs and taken them with her.

Just for the fun of it.

***

The last of her boxes were unpacked.

Liza's meager personal belongings were either neatly stowed away in closets or arranged on bookshelves and credenzas throughout her grandparents' house.

Her house.

She wasn't sure it would ever completely be *hers*, but she knew she belonged there.

Liza didn't bring much with her. The few items she'd deemed important enough to transport from Boston were sentimental and random. In fact, from the looks of some of the things she packed, Liza was now worried she might have unknowingly suffered from some kind of mental breakdown before she left. Her belongings had clearly not been chosen by someone who was in full control of their decision-making and cognitive skills.

For instance, she hadn't brought a single cup or plate or towel with her yet somehow managed to carefully pack the collection of foreign Coca-Cola bottles she'd gathered during their international travels. They were now artfully displayed on a library table in the living room.

She'd forgotten to pack any underwear (and, since all her drawers were empty when she left the house, had no idea where they were, which was a little disturbing) but *had* packed a box of nothing but melted candle wax that she'd collected from all the candle holders in the house. Yes, she liked to melt down the old and make new candles but why had she deemed *that* wax necessary?

And then there was the plastic bag full of more than three-hundred corks.

Still, she'd managed to bring every single item of clothing she'd ever owned, including the sweatshirt she'd cut the neck out of back in 1989 when she was just a kid. Well, other than her underwear. *That*, she'd managed to leave…somewhere.

"Liza Jane," she declared, her voice booming through the empty rooms. "You're a little pathetic."

The dryer buzzed in response, a reminder that she needed to change loads. The sheets and blankets on the bed were clean, but musty from non-use over the past few years. She'd spent the previous night coughing and sneezing. She wasn't ready to throw them out yet so she hoped a good dousing with Tide and that fabric softener with the annoying white teddy bear who was always laughing would help.

Momentarily forgetting her self-deprecating speech to herself, Liza scurried to the dryer to take action. With each thing she'd done that morning, she'd mentally hit Mode over the head with it.

He didn't think she could hack it. *He* didn't think she'd stay down there. *He* didn't think she could be alone.

Liza Jane was a stress cleaner. She enjoyed dusting, washing dishes, mopping, and organizing. It just wasn't cutting it today, though. The more she thought about Mode's phone call, the madder she got.

Thinking about Mode frolicking around her house with Jennifer did not help. Changing her locks. Ha! Like a lock could keep *her* out.

Mode would've known that, too.

Oh, he *knew* she was a witch. He was embarrassed by it, but he knew. "Just don't do anything out in public, okay?" He hadn't even had the decency to look ashamed or embarrassed when he'd asked.

"Like what, Darren?" she'd snapped. "Ride my broom? Turn the waiter into a frog?"

She'd looked at his face then and saw that it wasn't awkwardness of her abilities that had him humiliated, it was old-fashioned fear. He was afraid of her. She'd softened a little then and changed the subject after promising him she wouldn't make a public spectacle of herself.

Hours later something must have clicked inside and he'd felt guilty. As a peace offering, he'd brought her a broom, one of those old-fashioned ones that looked handmade and like it belonged by a storybook witch's door.

In fact, it *was* now standing by her front door. She was sentimental, after all. And it was a nice broom.

Still, his ideas never wavered. Two years later he asked her to move her altar out of their bedroom and into another room of the house. He claimed it was for the sake of "space" but she'd read him like a book. It was easy to do it by then. She only had to lightly press her thumbs together. She'd pressed them on his temples once, and then on his third eye, and they'd been connected ever since and would be forever.

Until *she* ended it.

"Well, shit," she sighed, looking around her living room again.

Her face cooled just a fraction and she closed her eyes to gather herself together again. She was angry at herself, angry for allowing him into this space, for making her angry *here*. Somewhere that had nothing to do with him. This space was meant to be hers and she'd all but invited him inside and asked him to throw darts at her.

It wasn't fair. Why couldn't her life be fair for a change? She'd given up years of it for his career. She'd helped put him through that last year of school, the year his parents died and their account (and subsequently his college funding) had been frozen.

She'd dropped out herself to work two jobs so that he could start his business and had then traveled all over the world with him so that he could work with the pop opera group and feel "fulfilled." She had put off having children because he wasn't ready, let her massage license expire so that he could have someone at home, kept the house clean, hired the maintenance workers, kept his records and balanced the checkbook, hid her magic and–

Liza, in the midst of her depressing and angry march down Memory Lane had not counted on the fact that the house could read her thoughts. She wouldn't make *that* mistake again.

Before she'd finished her last thought, two things happened at once:

The front door swung open from the pressure of a hearty knock...

And two of the foreign Coca-Cola bottles sailed off the shelf on the other side of the room, hovered dramatically in the air before proceeding to spin around uncontrollably, and then crashed to the ground, showering the living room with a thousand glittery shards of glass.

Liza, hand covering her mouth in embarrassment, was left staring at her visitor in shock.

"Um, hi?"

The curly-haired brunette holding a corning ware dish covered in aluminum foil gave her a baffled grin. "I'm your neighbor from the next farm over. Um, welcome to Kudzu Valley?"

Chapter Three

STILL EMBARASSED at her emotional display back at the house, Liza stomped through the library's double doors and exhaled loudly. Several people sitting in rocking chairs grouped together around the magazine stand glanced up at her from their periodicals, disgruntled.

"Sorry," she whispered.

It was obvious to Liza that Jessie Shelby, twentysomething housewife and casserole making extraordinaire, had tried to ignore the fact that she'd just seen her new neighbor make glass bottles dance around in the air and then crash to the floor using nothing but her mind. She'd chatted casually about the weather, asked about her mother, mentioned the new coffee shop going in downtown and had politely inquired about Liza's business venture.

In the end, though, after she'd patiently followed her into the kitchen and watched Liza place the broccoli and cheese casserole (topped with crumbled potato chips) in her refrigerator, Jessie just couldn't help herself.

"Did I just see you—"

Liza had mumbled some unintelligible reply without turning around but Jessie accepted the answer for what it was—confirmation. She knew better than to lie, although her younger self might have made something up to change the subject.

Jessie waited a beat and then continued her line of questioning. "Does that mean you're a—"

"Yes."

The awkward silence that followed was only interrupted by the old-fashioned clock on the wall, ticking away the minutes that seemed to stretch on forever. Liza continued to root around in the refrigerator while the other woman studied her from behind. She could all but feel the questions building in Jessie's mind, but a combination of fear and southern respect kept them at bay.

Liza sighed inside, disappointed in herself for making the other woman uncomfortable. She wasn't ashamed of being a witch, she'd never hurt anyone on purpose, and she'd just moved from an area that actually focused part of its tourism campaign on witchcraft. But the words her mother had told her the morning she set out for Kentucky still rang in her ear.

"Don't be talking about any of that stuff you can do," Mabel had warned her. "You just don't know how people are going to react and you don't need them mistreating you. Or worse."

"Oh, Mother. It's not like they're going to burn me at the stake. Besides, I don't just go around bragging about it or wearing a T-shirt. And anyway, Nana Bud was a witch," Liza had pointed out, feeling both small and defensive.

Mabel had let that one pass. "And she kept it quiet, too. Didn't go blabbing her mouth about it to everyone. Just do what you want, you always do, but don't say I didn't warn you!"

She was used to her mother's heightened paranoia about the people around her. Mabel was always convinced people were talking about her and excluding her from things with malicious intent. If Mode hadn't said something along the same vein, she might have just ignored her. But he'd also sent out a warning.

"Don't talk about witches while you're there!" his text had read.

Liza had been confused about the "while you're there" part. He still didn't believe she was going there to stay. But his words, coupled with her mother's, had made her nervous. She was in a politically conservative area. What if they mistook her for a devil worshipper or something?

Still, she *wasn't* going to hide it anymore. She hadn't practiced, not really, in years. And that had been hurtful, wounding to hide that part of her away. She liked her abilities, she enjoyed having powers, and she hated having to pretend to be something she wasn't.

No, if she was going to get off on the right foot in Kudzu Valley, she was going to have to be honest, even if it made both of them uncomfortable.

At last, Liza had turned around and studied the young woman standing before her. She was a perky little thing with beautiful curly hair and big green eyes. At the grocery store Liza had been surprised to see so many people wearing flannel pajama pants that dragged to the floor, their edges brown and frayed from the ground. She'd never seen such a thing before and it had taken her aback, making her wonder if that was the popular women's style in Kudzu Valley. (If so, she was out of luck. She wanted to fit in, but no way was she giving up her clothes.)

So now, as she took another look at her young neighbor, Liza felt a certain amount of respect for the woman's stain-free khaki pants, wrinkle-free pullover, and black pea coat. She wore little ladybugs at her ears and a matching necklace.

"It's a family thing," she'd explained to Jessie. "Kind of a legacy I guess you could call it; it's just something that's been passed down over the years. My grandmother was the same way, and my sister is in her own way, but they could always control themselves better. Sometimes I just let my temper get the best of me. I was thinking about something I really shouldn't have been and it just kind of...happened."

"Huh," Jessie had replied.

Liza couldn't judge the blank look on her face and felt it rude to violate her thoughts at their first meeting.

"I guess it's not that different than having a musician for a parent or an artist," she'd said, "and then getting some of that ability yourself. We're all different. I can't do all the things that my grandmother did and my sister can't do the things I do. But we all have a part of it."

Jessie nodded then, and didn't appear to be particularly shocked. "Yeah, people talked about Rosebud sometimes. I only seen her out in the garden when we rode our horses up here. She was always real nice. Others, though, they'd come up here when their kids were sick or they had some kind of problem that doctors or church couldn't fix."

Liza smiled. "She enjoyed getting company up here. I think she regretted not having a bigger family. She always liked taking care of people."

"My mom brought me up when I was eight. I kept getting these ear infections. Went up to Lexington and had saw a specialist. Had surgery and tubes and everything. Nothing helped. I'd wake everyone in the house up in the middle of the night just hollerin' my head off," Jessie laughed. "Drove everybody crazy. But my daddy brung me up here to see her. Said she was probably the only one who could help me. She sat down there in a rocking chair in the living room and pulled me up on her lap. I reckon I was four, maybe five. Anyway, Bud lit up a cigarette, brought her head close to mine, and blew smoke right in my ears. They never bothered me again."

Liza's nose began to twitch, a warning that her eyes might start to fill next. "She did that to me once, too. It was the only time I ever saw her smoke. She was a healer. That was one of her biggest strengths. I'm not *that* good, but I do it as well. I'm actually opening up a business downtown. I'll be helping people find natural remedies to things and giving massages and spa treatments. Would you like to go sit down in the living room?"

At first Liza had been a little uncomfortable at the idea of a stranger just showing up on her doorstep without an invitation and inviting themselves inside. But that had worn off soon enough.

The two women had spent an enjoyable hour talking about the town and changes it had seen since Liza and her family left.

They'd laughed quite a few times, seemed to share similar interests in music and movies (Jessie loved Jason Aldean but her husband called him "crap" and had refused to go his concert with her when he came to Rupp Arena in Lexington so Jessie had gone alone).

But even throughout the visit, Liza still got the distinct feeling that Jessie wasn't entirely comfortable. She could sometimes all but feel the other woman's nervousness and apprehension. Liza watched her as Jessie's eyes darted around the room, often landing on the bottles and studying them intently, as though just waiting for the moment when one would fly off the shelf and at her head. When Liza offered her a drink, Jessie had jumped up and offered to get it herself, overly eager to be accommodating.

Liza knew from experience that the apprehension would fade over time, but for some people it was never going to be possible for them to feel relaxed with their guard down when they were sitting in front of a person they thought could curse them for no other reason than they felt like it.

Still, Liza liked her new neighbor and hoped they could be friends. God, she needed friends. And she didn't think Jessie would be leading the rest of the townspeople with pitchforks any time soon, so that was something.

***

There wasn't much reading material in Liza Jane's house. Her grandparents' eyesight had gone bad way before she came along and the only reading material she'd found so far was a whole stack of Jackie Collins' novels and a *TV Guide* from 1993. Oddly enough, given how things eventually re-gained popularity, she could still find *The Facts of Life, Designing Women,* and *Dallas* on TV even now...the times were a little off, though.

The county library was contained in a single room that was only slightly bigger than her downstairs area. A block of computers were set up against a wall. There were eight seats in total, filled with men and women of various ages, all pecking quietly away at the keys.

A sign above the row of computers read:

For official use ONLY. Only job hunting and bill paying. NO games or social media!!!!!!

Liza paused to appreciate the irony that all but one of them were currently scrolling through their Facebook newsfeeds.

"Hi," she began in a quiet, but what she hoped was a friendly, voice as she approached the desk. "I need to see about getting a library card."

The middle-aged man on the other side of the desk looked up from a Styrofoam container containing what smelled like fried fish. He finished chewing, for which Liza was grateful, and studied Liza Jane with interest. His nametag read: Cotton Hashagen. He was hefty with shockingly red hair, huge front teeth, and a tie-dye sweatshirt with a picture of a chubby pig. The shirt read "Bobbie's Buffet Barn: Don't Stop 'til You're Happy as a Pig."

It listed a Kudzu Valley address.

Liza immediately thought of all the jokes comparing buffets to troughs and wondered if the owner had even considered that when naming their restaurant after a structure that housed farm animals.

Who was she kidding? That's probably why he'd done it.

"Can I see a photo ID?" Cotton finally asked as he deftly wiped his big, meaty hands on a tiny napkin and then daintily dabbed at his mouth.

Liza poked through the knock-off Coach bag she'd bought from a street vendor in Boston while Cotton sat by and watched her, occasionally huffing with impatience. "Here you go," Liza declared at last, sliding the card across the desk. She watched as the man glanced at it, brought it closer to his glasses, and frowned.

"Oh, I know," Liza said in a hurry, leaning over the desk and pointing at her picture. "I had black hair back then. I had that done back over the summer when I was going through my divorce. Got a tattoo, too. Cheaper than therapy," Liza joked.

Cotton did *not* look amused so Liza slowly let her own smile fade. "I'm back to my original red now. I promise that's really me, though."

Like he hadn't even heard her, Cotton held the card up to the light and examined it from all angles, as though trying to determine if it was counterfeit.

Yeah man, Liza said to herself. *Because there's obviously a lot of people who want to open fake library card accounts. It must be your biggest percentage of crimes here.*

She plastered the friendly, polite smile back on her face, though, and reminded herself that she was in a public place and not everyone appreciated snark. Still, she'd kind of thought that small town places would be a lot friendlier than their Big City counterparts. So far Cotton was *not* rolling out the welcome wagon.

"It's just that your address here says *Massachusetts*," Cotton replied sternly. He sent Liza a hard, withered look then, as though trying to determine what kind of scam she might be trying to run on the county.

"Yeah, well, I just moved back here," Liza explained. "I've only been here a few days so far and I am still trying to settle in and everything."

Cotton narrowed his eyes until they were thin little slits. "Do you have anything with your local address? A utility bill? Renter's contract? Cable bill?"

"I own my house," Liza said in return. "My grandparents left it to me." She had no idea why but now she was slightly miffed that the man would assume she was renting, although she wasn't sure why *that* would bother her. She'd been a renter until they'd bought their house and, up until recently, she'd been renting her condo.

"Well, I'm sorry but I just can't issue one without *at least* a photo ID with a local address," the insufferable man sniffed self-righteously, handing Liza back her card. Liza felt like she'd just been called out at the video store for trying to rent porn with a fake ID.

However, Liza Jane knew the surly librarian wasn't being honest with her as soon as their fingers touched. In a single meeting of skin, Liza was able to read his mind like a book, no pun intended.

She could feel the aggravation in her growing as she pulled herself to her full height and let her eyes bore into him. "Well that's not true, is it?" she asked, hardly recognizing her own steely voice. "There *are* things you can do for me today. For one thing, you can offer me a temporary card for thirty days, until I get my new license. I just have to leave a credit card number with you."

Lightning flashed through Cotton's eyes. "No ma'am," he sputtered, his face growing hard and her fingers tapping nervously on his desk. "We don't do that *here*. Now you'll just have to come back later. I can't do a single thing to help you."

Liza didn't know *why* this man was being so difficult and the simple act of checking out a book from the library so challenging. It was a library, for crying out loud. She was paying taxes there now, shouldn't she be allowed to check out books?

Furthermore, Liza couldn't figure out why the whole thing was making her so enraged, but she suddenly found herself more than mad—she was livid. This day had *not* gone as planned.

As Liza stood there and seethed inwardly, Cotton picked up a silver container, and took a sip from it, and then went back to his fish. It was clear that he was over Liza and had no intentions of continuing the conversation.

"Look Mary Elizabeth," Liza hissed, wanting to get her point across but still trying to remember the library manners and rules that had been ingrained within her since childhood.

Cotton looked up, a piece of white fish meat stuck to his bottom lip. "My name's not Mary Elizabeth," he said with a scowl. "My name is–"

"I know what your name is," Liza snapped. "It's from a book. Now you and I both know you can help me. For one thing, I know you did it for that man over there."

Liza gestured towards the row of computers where a portly man in a Cincinnati Bengals cap typed happily away on Facebook Chat. "You gave Eddy there a temporary pass and he's just here in town for railroad business. He doesn't live here at all; he's only going to be here for two weeks."

Cotton's eyes grew wide and his mouth dropped open as he quickly looked first at Eddy and then at Liza Jane. "Well I. How did you–"

Liza knew she should just let it go and go back another day but she'd taken it that far already. Might as well go the rest. "I don't know *why* you don't want to help me but I do know you have those contracts behind you in the top drawer of that black filing cabinet. It would only take a second, you'd be doing the right thing, and that would be the end of that. Do you really want me to call Phyllis?"

Phyllis, as Liza Jane shouldn't have known since that was the first time she'd ever been in the library, was the head librarian.

With his eyes still wide and mouth agape, Cotton was too stunned to protest. Instead, without taking his eyes from Liza, he stood, wiped his hands on a napkin and trotted over to the filing cabinet. He continued to watch Liza as he reached blindly into the drawer and pulled out an application form for a temporary card. He got the right form on the first try without even looking, which made Liza shake her head. She'd known all along that he could issue a card to her.

Neither Liza nor Cotton spoke another word to the other.

Ten minutes later Liza held a new library card in her hand. It was still warm from the laminating machine.

However, she'd somehow lost all interest in checking out any books.

***

So far the day had been a bit of a bust. So far she'd gotten herself riled up by her ex, destroyed some of her favorite bottles, freaked out her neighbor, and jumped onto the town librarian in front of a room full of people.

She hoped none of those things would hurt her place as resident healing therapist and day spa owner in Kudzu Valley.

To her annoyance, she'd gone to that buffet on Cotton's T-shirt and the waitress had refused to bring her a drink. Instead, she'd glared at Liza and made someone else wait on her.

And the fried chicken hadn't even been that good.

"Well, I can't go home," she muttered to herself as she turned onto Main Street. There was nothing for her to do at the house. She'd already unpacked, didn't have any books, and the internet guy wasn't scheduled for another three days. Back in Boston she might have dropped in on a friend or gone to the movies.

Well, that's what she would've done before the separation and divorce filings. Her friends had all kind of scattered after they'd learned she and Mode had zero chance of reconciliation, as though the divorce was an illness and might rub off on them. Besides, they'd been *his* friends anyway. She didn't win them in the custody battle.

Of course, she had zero friends in Kudzu Valley and the nearest cinema was an hour away.

"I'd like a cocktail please," she said to her steering wheel. "Oh yeah, can't get one here!"

She leaned over and turned the radio on, but the new artist was lauding the benefits of living in a small town and claiming that anyone who didn't appreciate it was just wrong.

Liza wasn't in the mood to rejoice in small-town life at the moment. Instead, she turned the music off and stared down the quiet little street in front of her, trying to decide what her next move was. She was at the greenlight that would allow her to turn left to go home or right to go eat somewhere and she was suddenly struck by a lack of motivation. It had been a long day.

Liza sat through three lights before finally moving. It was fine, though. Not a single vehicle drove in either direction the entire time she sat at the greenlight.

The town only had three fast food restaurants: a Taco Bell, Hardees, and McDonald's. Mode would've complained for the rest of the day if she'd so much as looked at a menu with him in the car with her. He took great pride in the raw vegan diet he'd been trying for the past year. That was one thing Liza couldn't get on board with, though. Sometimes she just needed a steak.

Now, however, nothing sounded better than a McChicken and caramel mocha. Cholesterol levels and waistline be damned. It wasn't like anyone was looking at her.

"Not like I'm trying to impress anyone around here," she sang cheerfully to herself as she zipped through the line.

She had her food beside her and was about to pull back out of the parking lot when the red sign caught her eye. "Well, hot damn!"

The town might not have had a Walmart or a cinema, but it *did* have a Red Box attached to the front of its McDonald's. She closed her eyes and thanked whatever franchise owner had the foresight to include such a beacon. There were few things Liza Jane enjoyed more than renting low-budget horror movies starring people nobody had ever heard of—Redbox's specialty.

Armed with some ghastly looking zombie films and a romance tearjerker from an author she didn't like to admit she enjoyed, Liza happily got back behind her wheel and zoomed away. She could handle another lonely night in the house as long as she had zombies and romance to keep her company.

"But not *The Wizard of Oz*," she told her caramel mocha before taking a sip. "That witch and those creepy-assed monkeys scared the hell out of me as a child and I still haven't gotten over it."

Liza Jane found her heightened anticipation of movie night at the house wearing off about five miles outside of town, however. It was barely 4:00 pm and she was already finished for the day, all ready to head back home and barricade herself in for the evening.

"Girl, you are one cat and tattered bathrobe short of being pathetic," she chided herself, shaking her head in disgust. "You need to figure something else out."

Up ahead, off to her left, she could see a sign that read "Lake Wilgreen" and without putting much thought into it, she made a quick exit from the country highway. She liked the water. Maybe she needed to hang out by it for awhile and regroup. It was important to get to know all the elemental signs, and not just yours.

Right away, the panorama view of the mountains on either side of her took her breath away. "Okay, now this is what I'm talking about," she said happily, trying to keep her eyes on the road and look at the same time. "I'm a country song!"

For awhile she'd been listening to songs about chilling on dirt roads, going for drives and parking on the dirt roads, spending the evening at the river side, having bonfire parties with friends…

There weren't many choices, though. It was either Top 40 (and she wasn't really digging the current trends), an out-of-place classical channel, farm talk radio, or what sounded like an excited preacher who never stopped to take a breath and ended every word with "a." Something was either wrong with the country station or her antenna; it wouldn't come in.

Liza did, however, have a stack of CDs in the passenger seat. Without taking her eyes off the road she let her mind shuffle through the titles until she landed on sunglasses-wearing Eric Church. Still dividing her energy between traversing the narrow country lane and opening the jewel case, she didn't break concentration until the CD had floated up from the seat next to her and dove into the awaiting slot. Only then did she release her breath and relax.

Soon, the lyrics of "Springsteen" were pumping through her car and, with her windows down, she sang along as loudly as she could, flat notes and tone deafness be damned.

"Huh, this is a lot farther than I thought," Liza murmured to herself as that song ended and faded into two more. She was enjoying the drive, but she'd been on it for awhile. Not much farther and she'd be in another county. Up ahead, Liza saw a gravel road and pulled into it. It didn't look like it went to a house or anything so she didn't think she was blocking a driveway.

Liza didn't have a map or a GPS so, with nobody else around, she turned the radio down, cleared her mind, and closed her eyes. She envisioned the road she was on and forced her eyes to travel down the winding pavement. She took in more barns, the rolling farmland, towering green mountains off in the distance, more burnt-out trailers and old farm houses...but she didn't see a lake of any kind. She traveled all the way to the end where the road literally made a dead end into a barn that was leaning precariously to one side.

"Well. Damn," she muttered. Now she'd have to turn around and go home, her little adventure over before it had begun. She was definitely going to stop somewhere and get a county map. She needed to learn about where she lived.

Still lost in her own thoughts, Liza had no awareness of the outside world and jumped when the hand tapped at her window.

The man who stood by her car, his knuckles inches from her window and a worried expression on his face, was in his mid-to-late thirties. He was tall, gorgeous, and more man than she'd seen in a *long* time.

His thin frame didn't look like it held an ounce of body fat. She might have been able to fit into his jeans (and wouldn't *that* have been fun) but what she could see was all muscle. His biceps were bulging under his stained white T-shirt and his rugged jeans molded perfectly to his strong-looking legs. He wore what appeared to be a real leather belt whose ends were held together by a shiny silver buckle—a picture of a horse head. More cowboy than Godfather.

She could see shocks of reddish hair poking out from under a baseball cap. The same fine hints of red were woven throughout the stubble on his darkly tanned face. He had perfectly straight, white teeth, although his mouth was currently set in a grimace of concern.

"You okay?" he hollered. His voice was muffled by the window.

Feeling silly, she rolled it down and turned her engine off. "Yeah, sorry," she apologized. "Am I in your driveway?"

She saw a four-wheeler parked a few feet from her car. Lost in her thoughts, she hadn't heard it pull up.

"This just goes up to the barn and livestock pond. I was headed across the way to my house. You having car trouble?"

"Oh, no, sorry. Just got, er, confused for a minute. I thought there was a lake out this way?"

It was his turn to look confused now. He scratched his head through his cap in bewilderment and then broke out into laughter. "Oh! You mean Wilgreen. Well, you see, that's kind of a joke around here."

"What?"

"Yeah, see, Clementine Wilgreen lives about a mile from here. He's eighty years old. Played the lottery, BINGO, whatever you got almost all his life. Said he was going to win one day and buy himself a big mansion on a lake."

"Yeah?" Liza prodded. A man named *Clementine*?

"Yeah, so anyway, he got himself a lottery ticket about five years ago. Told everyone it was the one. Went around town bragging about all the stuff he was going to buy when he was wealthy. Even filed divorce from his wife so that the old broad wouldn't get all his money when it come in."

"Did he win?"

The man grinned. "Sorta. He won $500. I guess that's a lot, especially considering he lives on Social Security. Hired a guy to come out and build him a pond and now he stocks it with catfish. That took all his money. Some of the fellows down at the Elk

Lodge felt sorry for him about the divorce so they put that sign up for him. You know, so that he can finally say he lives in a house on a lake."

Although she felt foolish for following a sign to a lake that didn't exist, Liza Jane laughed in spite of herself.

"That's just some small town humor for you I guess," he blushed. "You're not from here, right?"

"How did you guess?"

"The accent. The hair. The Massachusetts license plates…"

Liza found herself blushing now. "Well, I'm originally from here. I'm living in my grandparents' old house."

"Oh yeah. Rosebud and Paine. They were good people. Awfully sorry they're gone. So you're their granddaughter?"

"Well, one of them. But you won't catch Bryar down here any time soon. She lives in Brooklyn and to her taking a vacation or leaving town means going to Manhattan."

The man didn't look like he knew what in the world she was talking about but he smiled politely all the same.

"I'm Liza Jane Higginbotham, by the way," she said, holding out her hand to him.

"Colt Bluevine."

His hand was rough and warm as it engulfed hers. She winced as a bolt of electricity shot through her arm and made her fingers tingle. Colt jumped back a little, pulling his hand away. "Sorry about that," he said, wrinkling his brow. "I must'a shocked you or something. Could be my side by side over there. She's cranky."

Liza Jane didn't think it was the four wheeler's fault, though. She'd felt that bolt before, seen that flash of blue light.

Colt Bluevine was going to mean something to her, or already *had* in a time neither one of them could recall.

She'd have to investigate this further.

***

After three hard, cold, mind-numbing (and finger numbing since there was no heat in there) hours of work she had three separate piles: the boxes of things she couldn't use but wasn't ready to get rid of yet (those would go to the attic), the things she *could* use somewhere in the house (like the toilet paper), and the garbage. The whole left side of the room was cleared out, giving workers ample room to get to the window and do what they needed to do.

Her next project was to set up a space for herself.

She knew that she should really be focusing on the business that she was about to open, especially since she hadn't gotten the workers in there yet or even seen it empty herself, but there was nothing she could do to speed up that timeline. All she could do was distract herself at home.

Liza had spotted an extra television stand in the guest room and this she lugged across the hall on a rag rug, pulling the rug gently on the edge with a strong grip, careful not to scratch the floor. The television stand was solid oak and much heavier than she'd assumed. Twice, she'd pulled with all her might, really putting her legs into it like she knew you were supposed to, only to find her fingers slipping from the rug so that she was thrown backwards, her body sliding across the hall and hitting the door to her grandparents' old room.

On more than one occasion she'd stopped what she was doing and took stock of the situation at hand, shaking her head in disbelief and frustration. She was *alone*. She had little strength. She had something that needed to be done and nobody to help her do it.

She was a witch.

Granted, Liza was a witch whose abilities might not be all-encompassing but they were *still* present and formidable. Couldn't she just move it? Just lift it up, watch it sail gracefully through the air by invisible hands, and then wait (unharmed and breathing properly) as it settled into the place where it was meant to go? She'd fixed her porch, after all. There wasn't a real difference, right?

Liza, who had always had trouble saying no to her own arguments, raised her hands before her and closed her eyes, ready to move forward with the spell when she suddenly took a step back and stomped her foot.

"No! I will *not* do that. The porch was for my self-esteem, because I'd had a hard day. I can't fall back on this every time something's hard. I *will* take care of it myself," she swore, wiping a grubby hand across her cheek. "Other women live alone and do this crap. I will, too."

So, she'd gone at it again, cursing the unit and her foolish pride.

Once it was centered against the wall she slumped to the floor, panting.

"I seriously need to start working out," she gasped as the beads of sweat rolled down her cheeks. Then she began to laugh, an almost hysterical sound that carried throughout the house, disturbing the small animals that had made homes inside the walls. On and on she laughed, until she fell over on her side and clutched her stomach in agony.

"I hurt and I'm hungry," she laughed-sobbed. "I'm sore, I'm hungry, and I don't have anyone to help me with either one of those things."

Her mouth felt like the Mojave Desert inside. She thought she very seriously could've killed someone for a drink of something—anything. Her hair, normally her pride and joy, hung in dirty, limp clumps in her face, broken free from its bobby pins. And in her exhaustion, soreness, happiness, and hunger she thought of Mode and brought to mind the *many* times she'd been in bed with the flu or something and he'd brought her soup and orange juice to her in bed.

Not all the memories were *bad*. She didn't want to just think of him in a bad way; she'd loved him once, after all.

But why did the *good* memories hurt worse?

The TV stand might have been heavy but it was perfect for its intended use. The top, once the dust and cobwebs were cleared, would hold her altar cloth and handmade rosewood box with the Swarovski crystal encrusted pentagram (a girl *always* needed a little bling). The VCR shelf underneath (the stand was old enough to remember the pre-DVD player days) would store her "props" as she liked to call them: small boxes of candles, herbs, stones, and oils.

Liza didn't use a lot of props for her rituals but she *did* like her fire and scents. She thought a little color, heat, and fragrant aroma made things festive on the right occasion. Sometimes the ritual of setting it all up, organizing what she needed, and then using them in the correct order and for the proper reasons was soothing and allowed her to focus more clearly on her task at hand.

Liza Jane had always enjoyed the drama of certain things, even before she was a practicing witch.

Chapter Four

"*Y*OU DON'T *have* to make a decision right now, but we'd sure like to have you on that committee," Effie Trilby assured Liza for what felt like the hundredth time.

Liza had officially been open for one week. During their sessions, Liza had heard several clients complain about the "good old boy network" that supposedly ran Morel County. Liza didn't know anything about that, but she *did* know that Kudzu Valley's mayor was the size of your average ten-year-old, a seventy-two year old grandmother of thirteen and one of the most intimidating people she'd ever met.

Effie, who had been waiting impatiently for Liza at her own front door when she arrived that morning, was not only town mayor but also served as the president of the Morel County Historical Society, Vice President of the Women's Club, Treasurer of the Ladies Gardening Club, and chair of the annual Morel County Chestnut Tree Festival–held the first weekend of August.

After her brief introduction and generic "welcome to the community" speech, both said while they stood in the cold on the sidewalk and Liza struggled with the lock, Effie'd wasted no time in getting to the real point of her visit. There was no beating around the bush with this one and she'd let Liza know right away that she was not only invited to join the groups, but expected to.

"Rosebud was a dear, *dear* friend to me," Effie had proclaimed dramatically as she'd followed Liza all through the downstairs, trailing her as she turned on lights, lit candles, and set the music.

"She belonged to every organization and club we have here in Morel and she was beloved by everyone," she'd continued as she'd helped Liza slide the new clean sheet over the massage table. "You could always count on Rosebud to jump right in there and help out in whatever was needed. We've sorely missed her presence. *Sorely.*"

This last part was said with emphasis and directed at Liza. She knew what Effie was saying to her: She was saying that her Nana Bud had done more than her fair share of the work and they were all likely worn out from picking up the slack her departure had caused.

"Well, I *would* like to get involved," Liza admitted.

Effie pursed her lips and preened a little, the smug look of a woman who already knew she'd won.

"I wanted to say, too, that you've done a wonderful job with this place," she said, finally managing to take a breath and look around. "I need to come in and get some work done on my back."

"Just give me a call and I will work you in."

"I'd also like to say that we're all very impressed with the fact that you hired local workers to get her up to shape."

Liza nodded. "Well, I wanted to try to keep it local if I could. Do my part, you know, for the local economy."

Effie laughed. "Oh, yes, that. Well, we're all impressed that you didn't just, you know."

Effie threw her hand up in the air and waved it around, making a little "whooshing" sound as she did so.

Liza was amazed. Did *everyone* in town know what she was? How? At least she wouldn't have to go around revealing it. One less thing to do.

"So, may we expect you Monday evening?" And just like that, Effie was back on topic.

The town's most powerful woman barely reached Liza's shoulders, had a bluish tint to her gray hair, and wore dangling little rhinestone-laced turkeys at her ears. And she was awfully persuasive.

"I really justgot moved in and haven't had the chance to meet anyone yet," Liza said, "or even get settled. This is really just a 'soft opening' here at the business. I'm still trying to feel my way around. So I'm not sure if I could give you as much time and energy as you need."

"Oh, phooey," Effie scoffed, shaking her head so that the turkeys danced back and forth.

It was then that Liza realized Effie's cardigan and slacks continued the turkey theme. For some reason, that mesmerized her and momentarily got her off track.

"You're still a child," Effie insisted as she leaned towards Liza and grabbed her by the shoulder. Her hand was bony but incredibly stronger than Liza would've thought. She had what felt like a vulture's clutch on her and Liza wasn't sure whether she should laugh or try to throw her off. "You've got tons of energy compared to us old folks! You're still on your first legs."

"Not anymore," Liza laughed. "I learned that yesterday. Ten years ago I could have ran up and down Main Street all day in the heels I wore. After an hour here I thought I was going to die from the pain. I'm not the spring chicken I used to be."

"You'd be the youngest one with us, but I don't think that would bother someone like you," Effie hedged, eyes drilling into Liza's. "And the sad fact of the matter is, if we don't start getting some of these young folks involved then when my generation goes there won't be anyone to carry it on."

Liza nodded her head and tried not to wince as the other woman's long fingernails dug into her skin.

"Young people today, they don't care like they used to. You can't get these teenagers to do things in the community anymore. They want to be playing on their computers, talking to people in California or Japan when they don't even know the person who lives next door," Effie declared, her voice full of emotion. "Just breaks my heart, it does. Soon we're not going to be a community anymore at all."

Whether she'd finally caved in from the guilt trip or the pain, Liza finally found herself agreeing to participate in everything Effie threw at her. She'd signed some forms, diligently copied meeting times into her tablet's calendar app, and exchanged phone numbers.

And by the time the little woman sailed regally through her door, Liza even found herself chair of a committee.

She still wasn't sure *how* that had happened.

***

Liza Jane stood back and admired her new floors and the beautiful cherry shelves that lined the walls. She was itching to get started on the unpacking part but it was getting dark. She'd need to return the next day. So far she'd been doing treatments, but hadn't yet unpacked her products and started pushing *those* yet.

"I own a business, I own a business," she sang as she danced around, her boots echoing on the floor and filling the empty room. Outside, the cars whizzed by, windows rolled down and speakers blaring everything from Hank Williams Sr. to Kanye West and Bill Monroe.

Liza walked over to the one of the windows and placed her palm on the cool glass, careful not to leave any fingerprints or smudges; she'd just cleaned them. The streetlights were on and they cast a warm, rosy glow over the sidewalks. If she closed her eyes, she could almost imagine what downtown Kudzu looked like back in the 1960s and '70s, when the shops were full and the sidewalks busy. She was astute enough to know that those days were never coming back, but she hoped she could do her part to bring a little something to the town again.

Her own brand of magic.

"Careful Lizzie."

The voice, gruff and melodic, swept through the room.

Liza could feel the hairs on the back of her arms stand at attention. The voice, laced with cigarettes and the occasional shot of rum, was deep enough it could've been a man's. But it wasn't.

"Nana Bud?" Liza whispered and turned, expecting to see her grandmother standing a few feet from her.

The room was empty and still, but the light streaking in through the windows shimmered just a little in the middle of the floor. She knew she wasn't alone.

"Watch," came the voice again.

Liza strained her eyes and focused them on the point in the floor where the light beams gathered and became something nearly solid. A thick wisp of smoke rose from the newly-laid floorboards and drifted upward, fanning out like a flower as it gathered in strength and opacity. Liza took several steps towards it, unafraid, and watched curiously as her heart pounded in her chest.

Though she couldn't see her grandmother, she could feel her sweet, steely strength. The vision that eventually formed was startling, to say the least: the blood seeping into the ground, the screaming, her own face...But now there was a woman as well, a woman she'd never seen before. The woman lay on the floor, her face red and puffy and streaked with tears. Black lines ran from her eyes where her mascara had bled. Her blood-red lipstick was smeared across her mouth. Her ratty old coat was torn and stained with something dark. It was hitched up above her legs and pooled around her waist, revealing red underwear and a soft belly that protruded over the loose elastic. The woman cried out for someone, Liza couldn't make out the name, and then slumped back down to the ground.

"What does it mean Nana Bud?" Liza asked, frustration growing inside of her. "What do you want me to do?"

But the vision was already melting away. Liza knew the exact moment when her grandmother's spirit left because she was suddenly standing alone again, a chill in the air, and a sadness in her heart.

***

Since she was in the house for the night with nothing to do, Liza Jane decided to make use of her time and organize her altar. Maybe try a little ritual. She'd already moved everything to her new room, after all; she just needed to organize.

She'd made sure her altar box rode up front with her on the drive down, and had gone so far as to take it in the Charleston, West Virginia hotel room with her. It contained some of her most precious items and she wasn't about to let something happen to them.

Now, as the sun sank down over the mountains, turning them a chalky blue in the twilight, she sat cross-legged on the old shag carpet in her "office" and carefully unpacked the items she'd spent years collecting.

The altar cloth was one she'd made herself. It wasn't going to win any contests (not that there *were* contests for such things) but she liked it. It had a Celtic triple moon on one side and a triquetra on the other and the cloth was a beautiful shade of hunter green on smooth silk. She'd done her best with the embroidery–something she'd done during the monotonous hours on a particularly boring trip she'd made with the pop opera group when they'd visited Kanas City. Back when she was still "allowed" to travel with them.

She had three tall, thick white altar candles. She didn't particularly *need* three of them, that's just the way Kohl's sold them in their January sale. She removed one from the box and placed it on the television stand and packed the other two in a shoebox. This, she placed on the shelf below.

Next, she opened a different shoebox that held an assortment of tea candles and skinny little taper candles. Liza had them in all colors, from black to silver. There were several different candle holders to hold the tiny taper candles, too. They ranged from beautiful silver antique pieces she'd unearthed in flea markets and estate auctions to funky Art Deco style candle holders she'd picked up at Target.

Liza Jane wasn't a snob when it came to shopping; she was just as likely to buy something from K-Mart or the Dollar General as she was from Marshall Fields.

Altar provisions were kind of a personal thing for witches. She'd never used a chalice or bowl or ritual bell, for instance. She did, however, have a little brass cauldron she used for mixing herbs and oils and cherished a handmade wand a friend had created for her. It was made of a beautiful piece of Dogwood.

She'd always been drawn to the Goddess and tried to buy things with the feminine energy since they called to her. For that reason, she kept two statues of the Goddess on her altar and one in her living room. They helped keep her calm.

"Well," she admitted to an athame she unwrapped from purple tissue paper, "the Valium is also helping these days."

But the Goddess statues couldn't hurt.

She had one white ritual robe and two heavy cloaks (a winter-white one with rabbit fur and a deep burgundy for summer) and these she folded up and placed on a stool next to her altar. She'd never really been into the "costume" aspect of ritual work, although she knew some people who were.

Liza was more of a "sky clad" person herself, although Mode had been slightly uncomfortable about having a wife who thought nothing of standing naked in the middle of the room, chanting and playing with fire.

"For God's sake Lizey," he'd whispered on more than one occasion, "just don't go outside like that and make sure the curtains are closed before you turn the lights back on. We have neighbors!"

"Prude," Liza muttered even now, still a little stung at the memory.

She wondered how Colt Bluevine would feel about her wandering around the house naked...

At least she wouldn't have to worry about shocking the neighbors anymore.

"Nobody here to see me outside naked but the skunks and the deer," she said with glee, all but clapping her hands together.

Then she was hit by another thought.

"Do snakes come out at night? I'd better Google that..."

Now that she had all those acres it seemed a shame to waste them and not try to garden something. She'd been good at that in the past and there were a few different herbs she liked to use in a few of her rituals. These she kept in little crocheted sachets and stored them on the shelf. They included mugwort, angelica root, devil's root, and black cohosh. She also had a five-pound bag of beeswax pellets because, despite Mode's insistence that it was easier to buy things rather than make them, she enjoyed creating her own candles.

Crafting gave her something to do. She was a Pinterest fiend. In fact, she had a bumper sticker on the back of Christabel that proclaimed she'd #nailedit.

When everything was arranged just the way she liked it, Liza got up and trotted down to the kitchen. There, she fetched a dark ceramic bowl and filled it with water. Carefully, she took it back upstairs and placed it on the floor in front of her. She then turned off the lights and used wooden matches to light first her altar candle and then three blue taper candles.

The room was suddenly filled with dancing shadows and the sounds of small flames licking at the musty air. Thin slivers of black smoke rose slowly upwards, dissipating and disappearing before they reached the ceiling.

Liza Jane peeled off her blue jeans, socks, and underwear and folded them neatly by the door. She then pulled off her sweater, trying not to get the fabric caught on her hoop earrings.

She failed.

Naked from the waist down and with her breasts jiggling against her chest she hopped around, blinded by the angora sweater as she tried in vain to free it from the sterling silver.

"*Damn it*," she cried, ruining the relaxed and cheerful mood she'd tried to create for herself.

As hard as she might, she simply could not get it loose. It was either going to tear the fabric or rip her earring out.

Not wanting either to happen (the sweater had cost $75; she was damned if she'd ruin it before she even got to wear it more than once), she finally gave up and spun a little verse. Suddenly, she could see again as the sweater was gently untangled and the piece of clothing was smoothly lifted over her head and held high in the air. Sighing in frustration, she reached up and pulled it down, as casually as she might pluck an apple from a tree.

She hadn't meant to use magic that early; every little bit she spent took something out of her, making the next attempt less effective. And she wanted what she was about to do to be as helpful as possible.

With the candles burning brightly Liza lowered herself to the floor and crossed her legs. She placed the bowl of water inside her legs on the floor and situated the three blue candles around her. She then proceeded to offer a protective spell to the four corners of the room, encasing herself in their walls with a barrier of security.

Gazing intently at the water, she spread her arms out beside her, palms up, and opened herself to the air to welcome in the energy that was slowly gathering around her. She could feel her own power intermingling with the influence of the house, the energy left over by her grandmother, and the vitality from the candle's flames and colors. They were more than just symbols to her, after all; she derived strength from them. It didn't always come on as quickly as it was that night, but she'd found that working in a new place always brought on a little more force, as she and it began learning about one another.

Liza could feel her heart and mind opening; her chest swelled with happiness and potency and a slow smile spread across her face. With her eyes closed she offered up ancient words, as well as words of her own creation, and felt the air about her tremble.

She could almost get lost in that sensation, in the feeling that there was something big and magical in the world around her and she was a major part of it.

But she had business to attend to.

Opening her eyes now, she bent slightly forward at the waist and gazed back down into the bowl of water. The once smooth surface was rippling now, making small waves, much like the air in the room. Downstairs the refrigerator hummed, her cell phone played a Bon Jovi tune that signified her sister's call, and the microwave "pinged" (she'd forgotten to take out some noodles half an hour ago and now the darn thing wouldn't let her forget).

She blocked out all of these and focused only on what was before her.

At first, there was nothing but blackness—the color of the bowl mixed with the mountain water. But then it began to change little by little. She could see herself standing over a table, her hands shiny with oil. A woman was on her stomach on the table before her, her naked arms outstretched and a white sheet covering her lower half. Candlelight flickered.

Next she saw a party. Live music and cowboy boots on a dance floor. The smell of hay. Laughter. The room spinning around and around. Liza Jane was dancing, the shoulders under her arms strong and muscled. Colt's eyes gazed down upon her, a hint of mischief in them.

Liza felt a warmth spread through her stomach, something that had nothing to do with her candle ritual but nevertheless an ancient ritual that men and women had known since the beginning of time.

The scene suddenly changed, however, and became darker. Liza leaned closer to get a better view and then jumped backwards as the bowl filled with the scent of blood. She heard screaming, saw pain, and felt fear rising in her throat. A man lay on the ground, blood spilling from his mouth.

And Liza stood over him.

Chapter Five

DAYBREAK WAS amazing–when that daybreak meant the first morning of your first official opening day at work in your fist official business, anyway.

And ready just in time.

Opening time was 9:00 am but she'd been there for two hours already, nervous and antsy. She'd had her "soft" opening already but this was the real deal. All her products were out and everything.

Her first client would be there at 11:30 am and had booked a sixty-minute Reiki session. She had another one at 2:00 pm for a Swedish massage and then a facial at 3:00 pm.

"Man," she laughed, tossing her hair back and twirling around in a little circle. Little sparks of light flew out from under her feet and then rose into the air like dancing fireflies. She was already *booking appointments for the upcoming weeks.* "The ad I put in the paper must have really paid off!"

In all actuality, it probably had more to do with the town's sheer curiosity of her than anything else, but she wasn't going to let her mind go there. She'd rather believe that the sore, well-paying residents of Kudzu Valley were just people who needed a good rub down.

And the place looked good, too. Mode had chastised her, saying that she didn't really know what hard work was, that she used her magic to do all the little mundane things she didn't like, like clearing the dishes. But her building's beauty had nothing to do with magic and everything to do with good old-fashioned hard work and elbow grease. Her wood floors looked brand new from the wax she'd gently applied to them, her windows glistened with Windex, and the air was fragrant with the scent of warm vanilla and cinnamon from the candles she'd artfully placed throughout the downstairs.

Liza stopped twirling and bit her bottom lip, suddenly giving in to a bout of nerves. She was anxious, that was true. Her stomach did a flop and gurgled as a reminder. She'd spent part of the morning in the bathroom, trying to get herself together. Everything was ready and she knew that she was good at what she did, even if she hadn't actually done it professionally for several years, but she wanted to make a good impression on everyone. The people from the week before had been pleased with her work and many of them had already re-booked appointments with her but still...

If this didn't work for her, if she couldn't make it in Kudzu Valley, she didn't know where she'd go. Everything she had was *there*.

"Oh, screw yourself Modey," she muttered, trying to get the image of his condescending smirk out of her mind.

And *because* she wanted to make a good impression and was never completely satisfied with herself and what she did, Liza raised her arms high in the air and waved them back and forth in tiny circles. In the blink of an eye, the floors changed from smooth and clean to actually sparkling and the decorative throw pillows on the vintage settee in her waiting area plumped themselves.

Sometimes it was good for the morale to assure herself she still had the gift and could use it when needed.

Of course, the trouble with the magical cleaning was that it wouldn't last. It was an allusion, more or less, and couldn't possibly hold once her attention and focus were turned elsewhere. Still, it tickled her to be able to do it at all and for a moment, at least, her stomach settled down.

To be on the safe side, she popped another Tums.

***

Thanks for taking me in at the last minute." Taffeta "Taffy" Cornfoot's muffled voice rose from the bed she was lying face down on.

It was already 5:00 pm, and starting to get dark. Liza had noticed right away that it got darker faster in the mountains, like the hills blocked out the sun and cast it away once it was finished with it. Taffy, County Court Clerk and a grandmother to sixteen, had waltzed through the door ten minutes before Liza had planned on closing.

"I know I don't have an appointment but Patsy came in the office this afternoon just bragging about the massage you did on her and she just looked so relaxed."

Taffy lowered her voice then and glanced quickly around the room, her eyes darting to all the corners to ensure nobody was hidden in the shadows, listening. "And believe me, making that woman relaxed is nothing short of a miracle. I should know. I've known her for forty-seven years."

Liza, herself, remembered the other woman's bossiness, critical appraisal of everything she'd done to the place, complaints about the music and candle scents...until Liza had started working on her. Her tune had changed *real* fast then.

It might have had something to do with the bit of lavender oil she rubbed onto her and the lemon balm she'd slipped under the sheet by Patsy's head and feet. By the time Patsy left, she'd all but swooned out the front door, her eyes dopey and her doughy body languid.

Now Taffy, who'd spent ten minutes reciting the minutes from the town's last Rotary Club meeting in case Liza was interested in joining, was quiet and still under the modesty sheet.

Liza worked on her callused feet, puffy and swollen, and felt sympathy whenever she felt the other woman tremble slightly from the touch. She'd learned Taffy was diabetic and suffered from a lot of nerve pain. Her hypertension caused massive edema in her knees and feet and it almost pained Liza to touch them.

"But I'm still gonna work," Taffy had declared as she filled out the medical questionnaire. "I know some of these women can't wait to file Disability and get their money from the government but I ain't one of 'em. I will work until they roll my cold, dead body out of that court house. "

Now, Liza tried to imagine a big ball of light, bright and warm. She closed her eyes and could see it there, just on the back of her eyelids. It was brilliant, like the sun, and radiated heat that sent waves all the way down to her toes. She brought forth a healing chant her grandmother had sometimes used when Liza's legs were bothering her as a child.

"Growing pains" they'd called them back then.

When Liza opened her eyes, the ball of light was in the center of the room, hovering over Taffy's body. Liza let it glide up and down the woman's height, from the top of her head to her toes, taking time to pause at painful and inflamed joints and muscles along the way. Although it warmed her and soothed her aches, it never quite touched her, always stopping before it made contact with flesh. Once it had circled around twice, Liza murmured a few soft words and it disappeared, dissipating into the shadowy room and leaving nothing behind but some smoke tendrils.

Half an hour later, Taffy was all but flowing on her feet and walking much easier than she had when she'd entered the building. "I don't know how you did it but you did more for me than any of those pain medicines and nonsense do that they give me at the doctor."

"Oh, just what I learned in school," Liza said with a wave of her hand.

Taffy narrowed her eyes. "I suspect it's more than that but I'll let that go. *For now.*"

Liza walked Taffy to the door, unlocked it, and then paused. "Look, I don't want to overstep my bounds or anything but my grandmother was a diabetic and there were some things she used that helped with the swelling and some of the nerve pain. They're natural, but of course I'd need to make sure that they don't interact with any of the other medications you might take. That is, if you're interested," she added in a hurry.

Taffy nodded. "I surely am. I'd rather stick with the stuff that comes from the roots and trees than that crap they make up in a science lab. What you got?"

So Liza spent the next thirty minutes getting to do what she really loved but hadn't been able to do in a very long time—talk about herbal healing. She went over essential oils and carrying oils, pointed out herbs, explained the steps to creating a tincture…

The longer she talked, and the more interested Taffy appeared, the more pleasure Liza felt balling up in her stomach. She was afraid she'd be rusty when the time came, since she'd had no use for any of it in years, but the opposite was true—she felt more confident than ever.

"You certainly do know your stuff," Taffy remarked as Liza bagged her items. Liza, for her part, was glad she'd let Taffy stay when she walked in unscheduled. "Did somebody teach you?"

Liza paused, a sampler box of oils in her hand. She was surprised to feel tears prickling at her eyes. Perhaps the day had been more exhausting than she'd thought.

"It was my grandmother at first," she explained as she attempted to gather her composure before she embarrassed herself in front of a customer. "We only came down here a few times when I was growing up but I was always fascinated by her garden and what she called her 'medicine room.' I'd ask a ton of questions, probably pestered her to death."

"Oh, shew," Taffy scoffed, patting Liza on the hand. "That's what grandmothers like. Did she teach you then?"

"A little. They came up to see us a lot, once they figured out Mom had no intentions of coming back. I went through a stage where I didn't care at all and didn't want to know anything about it, but then it turned around again in high school. She was a good teacher," Liza said simply. "She knew what she was doing."

"That she did, that she did," Taffy murmured in agreement. "Did you do any formal studying?"

Liza nodded. "I did, actually. I couldn't find a college program that I liked so I went pre-med. I figured I would need to know about western medicine, too, and those classes gave me all the science and biology I was lacking. I interned for a naturopathic doctor in Boston for a year and loved it. But I didn't graduate."

"Oh, I'm sorry. What happened?" Taffy's cheeks turned bright pink then and she lowered her eyes. "I'm sorry. That was nosy and rude of me. I am a nosy and rude old woman."

Liza laughed. "No, it's okay. Just embarrassing. No big story or anything; I just met my husband, fell in love, got married, and that was the end of my own personal life for a very long time."

Taffy nodded, understanding clouding her eyes. "It's very hard to be a woman sometimes. I don't think a man can ever realize how much we give up, even when it's not necessary to let it go. When a woman has committed herself to a family, and I don't just mean children but to the idea of belonging to something she has to nurture, she can never truly belong to herself again. She can't turn that little button off inside her head. Men are different."

"You got that right," Liza agreed, but she was taken aback by Taffy's words–words she strongly identified with. For years she'd done little for herself, other than getting the massage license she only briefly used and the job at the nonprofit that she'd lost during the separation.

Mode had been able to keep his career, leaving her alone for weeks at a time, indulging in his hobbies (some of which were blond haired and blue eyed) and having a completely separate life apart from their marriage.

She hadn't been able to.

That worry, that constant *need* to make their house just right, to keep their marriage fresh and exciting, to take care of his emotional and physical needs...those things had overpowered her.

"Hey Taffy?" Liza asked suddenly as she handed Taffy her bag of purchased items. "Did you ever roll over in bed, first thing in the morning, and look at your husband and feel totally disgusted? Like, the first thing that goes through your mind is, 'I'd kill you right now and take myself on a three-week cruise through the Bahamas with the insurance money if it weren't for the fact we're laying on the nice sheets I just bought and I don't want to ruin them'? Do you ever feel like that?"

Taffy grinned and patted Liza on the hand. With a twinkle in her eye she leaned in close and replied, "All the time, dear. All the time."

***

When the doors were locked, the towels and sheets gathered from the laundry basket and bagged up to be taken home and washed, and all the candles blown out Liza Jane did a little happy dance across the floor.

"I survived my first *official* day!" she sang, doing a little jump in the air and clicking her heels together. When she missed the landing and ended up sprawled on her bottom she just laughed and laid back on the floor.

As she'd known it would, the wood had lost its luminosity as soon as the first customer had arrived and she'd busied herself with them. But it didn't matter; they still looked and smelled good.

"I am a business owner," she proudly told the ceiling, though it didn't appear to be impressed.

She was disappointed, of course, that she'd spent her opening day alone, without the presence of any loved ones. Her mother *could* have come down. For that matter, her sister could've come as well. It may have only been a couple of rooms in an old building where she gave massages and facials and sold herbs but it was still a big deal to her.

She'd known nothing about running a business going into it and had spent months studying books and websites and teaching herself the ins and outs of bookkeeping and marketing.

Liza felt pretty darned pleased with herself.

It was late, however, and she needed to get home. Liza picked herself up off the floor, dusted her bottom, did one last walk-through to make sure everything looked okay, and grabbed her purse and keys.

She couldn't wait to get to the house, make herself a hot chocolate (with a dash of Bailey's because she'd earned it) and slip into bed. She already had four appointments scheduled for the next day, although the day after just had a facial so far. She was a little concerned but hoped that word of mouth would eventually help bring her a steady clientele. It would be Christmas soon and some of the businesses in Kudzu Valley were having holiday open houses. She planned on having a big "Grand Opening Holiday Open House" then and would be prepared to mingle, network, hold a raffle, put out cookies, and whatever else it was she had to do to get people to walk through her door and spend their money.

Oh, but Christmas. Liza groaned to herself as she locked the door and gave it a test tug.

What the hell am I going to do for Christmas, she thought as she headed to her car. *I won't be so pathetic that I will eat alone.* She'd already done that for Thanksgiving.

Her mind was still pondering the Christmas predicament when she felt something behind her. Nothing had made a sound, and nothing had moved at all, but Liza was still aware of it. The presence of someone who didn't need to be there tickled at the back of her neck, giving her what her grandmother had called "the willies."

Liza didn't pause or quicken her pace, but she *did* become more alert and aware of her surroundings. She'd parked behind the building, in a gravel lot that ran the length of the street and faced the river. Christabel was the only vehicle. Key in hand and ready, without removing her purse from her shoulder she undid the lock and jumped inside in one swift movement.

With the door locked, the engine started, and her headlights on she turned off the "woman" part of her and turned on the "witch."

Other than the spotlight her headlights made in one spot on the old brick at the back of the buildings, the whole length of the street was dark. The moon, hidden by the clouds, offered no illumination and the streetlights only faced the road out front. The shadows were dark and murky.

Liza saw *him* then, a man. He wasn't hiding, exactly, but he wasn't doing anything to make his presence known either. The tall, figure leaned against a dumpster, the bottom half of him lost in the darkness. He was looking at her, she could feel that, and it made her uneasy.

"Don't be paranoid," she warned herself. "This is his town, you're a newcomer, and Kudzu Valley is not a violent place. You're too used to being in the big city."

Her words did little to settle her nerves, however, because she knew that he'd had impure intentions towards her when he'd seen her. She could feel them even now, radiating from him like radio waves and traveling the distance between them until they closed in on her.

Jerking back a little, Liza fought to remain in control. There was a stickiness about the hatred and anger he projected at her. He didn't just dislike her, she repulsed him.

But *why*?

Closing her hand around the talisman her grandmother had given her many years ago, and one that rode in the front seat with her at all times, Liza sent her mind out to him, seeking answers. She got nothing in return but a fiery black wall, palpitating with heat and frustration.

Sometimes she wasn't able to see anything, especially when it concerned something personal to her. That was a sad fact about her "gift"–she never seemed to be able to help herself much.

But while she might not have been able to make any sense out of *why* he was there and what he wanted, she was able to see his face. The smooth complexion, except for the ruddy mole on his cheek, shockingly red hair, hefty build, and the "Will Work for Weed" T-shirt that was partly hidden behind his flannel coat could only belong to one person.

Cotton Hashagen.

But that made zero sense. Cotton was just a *librarian.* Sure, they'd had a tiff during her first few days but he would've been over that by now, right?

He wouldn't hurt her. He had no reason to.

Chapter Six

LIZA FELL BACK against the wall in her treatment room and tried desperately to get herself together for what felt like the fifth time.

"The sheets too? Did it have to be the sheets?"

She'd ordered those sheets from Macy's website. They'd cost $135, more than twice what the sheets on her own bed cost. She'd loved them so much that when she'd first opened them to put them on her massage table, she'd pressed her face against them, marveling in their softness.

Now they were ripped to shreds and hanging artfully over the privacy screen in the corner of the room.

Her business was completely trashed, from corner to corner. Nothing had been left untouched.

Well, at least on the first floor anyway. Whoever had done it had apparently not had time to make it upstairs.

The woman in Liza wanted to drop to the floor and cry and cry. Nothing of value had been stolen. After all, there wasn't much street value in aromatherapy candles. It had been a personal attack.

The witch in Liza wanted to go apeshit and fly through the roof and seek revenge. How *dare* someone come in and upset something she'd worked so hard for?

Liza knew that with some careful thoughts and planning and with the right tools and a whole lot of energy she could have everything back together in a matter of hours. Well, most everything anyway. The things she knew how to fix.

Part of her wanted to go ahead and do that. Wanted to go ahead and make everything right so that she wouldn't have to stand there and look at the mess and could continue on with business as usual.

And then, after she closed, she'd march home to her altar, see who was responsible for it, and throw something so hard at them that they wouldn't know which end was up for the rest of the month.

But that wouldn't have been the right thing to do. She *needed* to go through the proper channels. She needed to treat this the same way anyone else would.

In resignation, Liza pulled out her phone and began dialing the police.

***

"Yep, looks personal to me." The detective, a man named Kroner, stood in the middle of the room with his hands on his hips and surveyed the mess. Other officers walked around, gingerly making their way through the debris, taking pictures and making notes. "You piss anyone off lately?"

"Apparently," Liza muttered.

"Anyone specifically?"

Detective Kroner had whistled and laughed a little when he'd first walked through the door. Liza had not appreciated that. It might have just been a few candles and oils to him, but to her it had been the beginning of a new life.

"I just moved here. I don't know enough people yet," she replied. She sat on the stool by the counter, the safest place in the room. If she'd stood anywhere else, she would have been ankle deep in wreckage. "I haven't been here long enough to make anyone *this* mad."

Detective Kroner looked down at his tiny little notepad, grumbled something to himself, and made a note. He did that after everything she said. She was thinking about saying a bunch of really random things, just to make him have to write more. So far, she had not been impressed by the justice system in Kudzu Valley.

For starters, it had taken two hours for the police to arrive, despite the fact the police department was across the street and she could literally see it from her front window.

And then there had been the laughter.

"There was a waitress who wouldn't serve me a drink," Liza offered helpfully. "But she just glared at me. I don't think it was her."

"Anyone else you can think of?"

"Cotton Hashagen," she answered at once. "I saw him lurking around out back when I got in my car. He looked like he was up to something."

"Cotton?" Detective Kroner laughed and snapped his notebook shut. "Naw, I don't think he'd do anything. I went to school with him. Good kid, great football player. Could've made something out of himself but hurt his leg senior year. Real shame..."

And that was how Liza's morning went.

***

The detective's words kept repeating themselves over and over in her mind, like a single line of a song on a broken record. "Gotta keep the temper in check, old girl," she reminded herself. "Gotta stay calm. Stay calm. Bad things happen when you're not calm. Bad things happen when you let it loose."

Liza continued to speak soothingly to herself while she folded the sheets and put another load of towels in. She could feel her heart pounding erratically under her skin and her blood was all but boiling throughout her veins. When she passed a mirror and caught her reflection, she wasn't surprised to see that her face looked sunburned, beet red from what she assumed was her skyrocketing blood pressure.

She wasn't a child or teenager anymore, though; she was an adult.

She *had* to learn to control her temper. If she couldn't, then she couldn't do any magic anymore. That had been her rule and threat to herself and she knew it was absolutely necessary.

Liza wore her emotions on her sleeves. She was sensitive. For a long time she'd tried to change that, to be someone else. Someone safer. But then her grandfather, of all people, had told her it wasn't necessary.

"Sugar bee," he'd said out of the blue one day while he was reading the paper, "you gots to take the good with the bad. If you lose your bad sensitive side, you lose what makes you good, too."

But she still needed to learn control.

Before she knew she was a real witch with real power, back when she was thirteen and full of raging hormones, she'd accidentally set fire to a hay bale. She'd been with her mother and stepfather, Gene, up in New Hampshire, at a bed and breakfast called the Wander Inn. They'd been there for a week, horseback riding and going for hayrides and such.

It was late September and her stepfather was doing some kind of Rite Aid thing. Liza Jane had met a fellow teenager, a boy named Tracy Coffey. He was also staying there with *his* parents and they'd bonded over mutual teenage boredom and a love of Nine Inch Nails.

By the end of the second day they'd played two games of checkers, watched an episode of "Saved by the Bell" in the common room at the inn, and exchanged phone numbers. After dinner that night she'd spent more than two hours making him a mixed tape and was out looking for him to give him the treasure when she'd rounded the barn and caught him in a lip lock with her sister.

Every emotion she'd ever been capable of had burst forth from her at once: anger, jealousy, betrayal, disappointment and, that one emotion that every teen experiences at the height of their hurt—overwhelming despair.

"Tracy Coffey!" she'd screamed. He and Bryar had looked up, guilty as rats in the cake batter. Her *sister* had the audacity to look ashamed as she quickly checked her blouse to make sure there weren't any gaping buttonholes. She'd been twelve at the time. Bryar had started everything earlier than most.

They'd both started towards her then but the scene had blurred through tears and anger. She'd thought she would boil over from the *bigness* of it all. And then the hay bale had shot up in flames, like someone had doused it with gasoline and thrown a torch on it. It had taken fifteen minutes to get it under control. As soon as it tapered down from the gallons of water being tossed at it, it would shoot right back up again.

The fire didn't go out completely until Liza Jane stopped her crying which, incidentally, hadn't stopped until she'd seen the look of terror on Tracy Coffey's face. That had, somehow, made her feel *much* better.

She'd received a phone call from Nana Bud the next morning.

"Liza Jane Merriweather, you need to control your feisty little britches," the voice, old but not frail, had warned her.

"What Nana?" she'd asked, still a little uncertain as to what her actual role in the event had been.

"I seen what you did to that hay."

Liza had felt her face flush with embarrassment. "They said someone put a cigarette out in it, that it was dry."

"Horseshit," Rosebud had scoffed. "You got yourself in a tither and directed all your energy at it. And now it's high time to learn what you are and what you can, and can*not*, do about it."

She'd had her first lesson in control that night. It was also the night she learned that she was a witch, and not the only one in her family. She'd had a few minor lessons along the way, but it was finally time for her to sit still for the big one.

She'd had a few hiccups along the way, but now Liza tried to control herself when she could.

She still hadn't learned much control, although she *did* pride herself over the fact that both Mode and Jennifer Miller *and* the Starbucks girl were all still alive. And human.

***

It had been a...*interesting* day to say the least. Liza was more than ready to get home. She'd spent hours at the police station, talking to the detective again.

That hadn't gone anywhere.

There was a gas station before she reached the turnoff to her road and she stopped there, first. She was out of caffeine at home, which would've been a real travesty considering the day she'd had, and she could use bread and sandwich makings.

The icy weather had brought others out as well so the store was unusually crowded when she walked in. It had been her go-to place for essentials since moving in so she knew which aisle she needed to visit. It didn't take her long to shop.

With arms full, Liza approached the front and stood in line. And ended up right behind Cotton Hashagen.

Ignore him, ignore him, ignore him, she chanted to herself.

But then he turned around, saw her, and flashed her a smile that was so smug, so condescending, and so much like Mode's that she'd lost it.

"I *know* it was you, Cotton," she exclaimed, not even bothering to keep her voice down.

"What?" he asked innocently, looking around at the rest of people who were starting to stare and giving them a "women, what do you do?" look.

"You trashed my store! You ruined my things!" she screeched. "I saw you hanging around outside my door!"

Cotton's face reddened and his eyes darkened as he stepped back from Liza. Everyone else had already taken their own steps back and were looking at her a little nervously. She was unaware of the fact that the hair around her face was flying outwards in her anger.

"If you come near my business again Cotton, I will kill you. Do you understand? I will *kill* you." Though she said the words softly enough, someone standing behind her gave an audible groan and there was a massive shudder that went through the crowd.

Then, forgetting her snacks and drinks, she left the building.

It wasn't until she was back in the car and turning onto her gravel road that she realized she'd shoplifted.

***

"We're just going to pretend that most of that didn't happen today," Liza Jane grumbled to herself as she turned onto her road. It was five miles to her driveway from there. Her driveway was nearly a mile long itself, and gravel. It was going to be a pain in the ass to get out when it finally snowed. Shit. She really hadn't thought about that. How was she going to get out? How had her grandparents managed it?

"They didn't," she answered herself as she passed by a yard inexplicably full of topless toddlers. Shouldn't they have been cold? The toddlers, that was, not her grandparents. Although they'd probably gotten cold as well. "The older people knew how to do it right. They froze enough meals for three months, chopped firewood, and hunkered down."

She wasn't going to be able to do those things. Plus, she *had* to get out. She enjoyed her own company but she'd go stir crazy. And she'd still have to earn money to pay the bills.

Liza went over recent events in her mind.

First, there was the phone call from Mode. That had gone...swell.

And then there had been the visit from her neighbor, Jessie. Jessie seemed like a nice enough girl but Liza was afraid she'd terrified her with the bottles. Who knew what she would go off and repeat? By the time she finished with the story, Liza Jane would probably be flying her furniture around the room while she stood in the middle and stuck pins in a voodoo doll.

Of course, if she were a different kind of witch, the voodoo doll would definitely have come in handy with Mode and Jennifer Miller...

"I should've just erased her," Liza sighed, still thinking of Jessie.

It was true; there were ways that she could've made Jessie forget what she'd seen and heard. Liza saved those spells for special occasions, though. The universe liked to work in balance. For every *one* thing that happened, *another* thing had to occur to even it out. She'd learned that when she erased someone else's memory of something, she herself lost a memory. If she were lucky it would be something like ever having married Mode in the first place. She was never that lucky though. More than likely it would've been a nice memory.

Like when she lost her virginity after prom on the picnic blanket on Revere Beach when she was seventeen.

(It was a lot more romantic at the time.)

Then she'd lost her temper at the library.

"I ought not to have done that," Liza sighed with regret. "Way to network with the locals. And get my business trashed."

"I promise I'm not always this moody and unstable!" she shouted at the scenery that passed her by. "I'm usually pretty normal!"

Then her business had been trashed.

Of course, there was also the lake that wasn't really there. In hindsight, she was embarrassed and a little upset that she hadn't known about the not-there lake as soon as she turned onto the road. Her senses weren't as sharp as they used to be. She needed to fix that.

Then again, she *had* met Colt. That was something. Those cowboy boots, those eyes, those *hands*...

"Too soon, Liza Jane, too soon," she warned herself as an image of Mode, smug and self-assured, flashed before her eyes. "You're not even divorced yet."

Like that had stopped him, another little voice spat.

Well, *she* was going to take all the time she needed to get her act together. She'd settle into the town, make some friends, re-open her business, and *then* she might start thinking about dating again.

"The detective is useless but I guess the day could've been worse," she admitted as she took the last turn onto her gravel driveway. "At least I have a little bit of money, my health, my house, and a car."

Her car bounced a few feet over the tiny rocks before giving a shudder, making a loud "popping" noise and coming to a complete stop. She listened in horror as the engine died and went silent. Nothing surrounded her but the overgrown dogwoods and sycamores and the sounds of birds calling to one another (*probably making fun of her*, she thought).

Liza Jane knew nothing about vehicles. She couldn't fix things she knew nothing about, not even on her best day. Still, she tried to envision the car starting, tried to see it rolling smoothly towards her house. Despite her ignorance, it *did* sputter for a moment but then went dead as a doornail again.

It wasn't going to happen.

Letting out a string of curses that would've made a sailor blush, Liza grabbed her purse, keys, and light jacket and jumped out of the car, slamming the door behind her in resentment.

It was a mile to her house. She wished she was wearing better shoes.

Welcome home, she thought wryly as she began the long walk, her thin spiked heels disappearing in the gravel, sending up clouds of white smoke.

Welcome home.

Chapter Seven

DRUGS," BRYAR ROSE declared with authority. "Had to be. He was probably waiting for a pick up or something. Then he saw you and trashed your store as a warning. You should carry some mace with you."

"The other day I was wondering if I should get a gun," Liza admitted.

"A *gun*?" Bryar scoffed. "You'd blow your damned foot off."

"I'll probably just start parking around out front from here on out," Liza sighed, hating the fact that she'd let someone spook her so much. "I *know* it was him…"

"I can take a look if you want," Bryar suggested. "Let you know what I see?"

"No, that's okay. I'll be fine."

Long ago both had promised to stay out of the other's business, at least where their magic was concerned. If they wanted to know something then they'd have to do it the old fashioned way—pry. They were close to one another, but boundaries were important. So was trust. Liza knew that her sister wouldn't do anything unless Liza told her she could. And vice versa.

"Although I still think you should've let me curse Mode," Bryar grumbled on the other side of the phone.

They might have promised not to involve the other in any ritual work or violate any boundaries where their thoughts or dreams were concerned, but they were still sisters.

"If you'd done anything to him it would've come back on you, and even worse," Liza said. "Need I remind you of Emily Tingly in the seventh grade?"

"Yeah," Bryar shuddered dramatically. "Let's not do that again. I'm even more attached to my hair than I was then."

When the middle school basketball star had dumped Bryar for Emily, the only girl in school with breasts, Bryar had taken her revenge female-style. Knowing that she was getting her hair permed the next day, Bryar thought she was being clever when she'd locked herself in her bedroom and thought up a hex in which the perm not only left poor Emily with a big ball of frizz on her pretty little head, but had turned most of it into an extremely unflattering shade of orange.

Emily had been mortified, inconsolable to her friends.

But Emily hadn't been half as upset as *Bryar* was when her alarm went off three days later and she discovered that more than half of her hair stayed behind on her pillow when she crawled out of bed.

It had taken more than a year for it to grow back, and according to Bryar, she still had a few bald spots.

***

"It is going to be a *good* day today!" Liza Jane lectured her reflection in the bathroom mirror later that morning. "I don't care what happens. It's going to be a good day."

Yes, someone had tried to ruin her. Yes, she'd somehow made an enemy and didn't know why. But she was determined to be positive, to have a new outlook on life.

The fact that she didn't have a vehicle to get her to town was a problem, of course. She'd walked back down the road to Christabel again, hoping for some wild reason that letting it rest overnight would somehow rejuvenate it, but the car was still as dead as it had been the night before.

"Stupid," she'd muttered to herself on the long walk back home. "It's not like the car just needed a little nap."

First things first, after she brushed her teeth and put on her makeup she used her phone to call information for a local garage. Of course that had gone over like a lead balloon. It was the automated operator and her combination of country/northeastern accent.

"City and state please?"

"Kudzu Valley, Kentucky." (It started out well enough.)

"What listing?"

"A garage."

Pause

"You're looking for 'Garden City.' There are currently no listings for Garden City in your area. Would you like to try another option?"

"Not 'Garden City.' Garage. *Mechanic*." (Now she was growing impatient.)

"Thank you. One moment please."

Liza Jane had waited.

"There is one listing for Mayfield Landfill. The number is—"

"No!" Liza had shrieked. "A *mechanic*."

"One moment please."

Liza started pacing around the room. –

"There is no listing for Mountain Knife Works. Would you like to—"

"Operator! Operator!"

Even with a live person on the phone it had taken several tries to get what she needed.

She wasn't going to let that get her down, however. It was going to be a *good* day.

Information provided her with three numbers. Nobody answered at the first one. It didn't even go to a voicemail. The second one told her it would be at least two weeks before they could get to her car and she'd have to find her own way to get it to them.

By the time the third one picked up, Liza was on the verge of panic.

"Jimmy Dean's Autos," the gruff voice on the other end of the line barked.

"Hi, I'm new to town and I live really far out and my car stopped running. I don't know what's wrong. It's just dead. I need someone to look at it and I also need them to come and get it. Do you all do that?"

"Nope, sorry," the voice barked again. "You'll have to bring it to us."

"Yes, but see," Liza did her best to keep her voice level, even though she felt like screaming. "I can't *get* it to you. It won't start."

"We don't got a tow truck," the man laughed. "So unless you want to push it…"

"I'm twenty miles outside of town," she lamented.

"Best get started now then," he laughed again. "We close at five."

And then, though she knew it was wrong, she turned on a charm of a different kind. Covering the speaker with one hand, Liza closed her eyes and muttered a few words her own grandmother had shared with her and advised her to only use when it was an absolute emergency. Liza felt the word could be used to describe her current situation.

She could feel the air around her changing, growing warmer. The tiny hairs on her arms stood at attention. The blood inside her churned and bubbled until she felt like she might explode and then a wave of goosebumps rippled across her skin from head to toe.

When she opened her eyes she could hear Jimmy Dean talking on the other end of the line.

"Well, I reckon we can come up there and get you. I can borr-y a truck and chain from a fellar I know. Where'd you say you was at? Can't leave a woman up in the mountains all by herself."

And with that, she had a ride into town.

***

It didn't take much for Liza to talk Jimmy Dean (an ancient man with unnaturally bright dentures and a shock of white hair) into dropping her off at her building. After all, it was only three blocks from the garage.

"Just come up here in about an hour or so and I'll try to have an answer for you," he promised as she hopped out of the cab.

She was hoping that not only would he have an answer, but that he would tell her the car was ready.

"Please let it be something like a bad battery," she prayed aloud as she dug around for the keys and attempted to let herself into the building.

She'd underestimated how depressing going back into work was truly going to be, however.

Her business was a mess. She'd tried to convince herself that it would somehow be better today, that she'd exaggerated it in her mind. That when she actually saw it, it would be fine.

She'd been right the first time. It was a disaster.

After walking around and letting out a string of expletives that would've made sailors run from a bar, and stomping her feet a few times, Liza sat down on her settee (surprisingly unharmed) and screamed as loud as she could.

That actually felt pretty good.

There was no doubt about it. She'd need some professionals to help with some of the bigger things. She could only magically fix things that she knew something about. She could, for instance, straighten a post on her front porch but she couldn't exactly build a porch herself.

For the next hour she sifted through the debris and threw away the items that couldn't be fixed: broken glass from candle holders, shreds of paper from flyers and brochures, and crushed light bulbs.

There were some things she was able to fix with a little willpower and inner magic: her torn afghan, a broken chair that was only missing a leg, a few floorboards that had only been partially pulled up...

By the time she was finished, her business was still a mess but looked far more presentable than it had when she walked in. But she'd need someone else to do the rest of the work. Things she didn't know about.

Liza was on her laptop (thankfully she took it home with her every night so nobody had bothered *it*) when the door opened. Liza looked up in surprise; everyone knew she was closed. She'd called and rescheduled every client who had an appointment for the next week.

Taffy entered, however, with flushed cheeks and a red nose, bringing a tuft of cold air in with her.

"Did you hear the news darlin'?" she asked in excitement before she'd even reached Liza Jane. "Did you hear it? It's all over town."

"Hear what?" Liza asked. She'd been on her computer for the past half-hour, making a list of items lost for insurance purposes. And before *that* she'd been cleaning. She hadn't seen or heard from anyone all morning, save her sister, the telephone operator, and Jimmy Dean.

"Cotton Hashagen," Taffy cried, eyes glistening.

"Did he get arrested?" Liza asked with glee, rubbing her hands together. Maybe she'd been wrong, maybe there was some justice in Morel County.

"No, oh no," Taffy replied, leaning in close to Liza. With her head lowered and her breath coming out in short bursts she whispered, "He's *dead!*"

Liza jumped back nearly a foot into the air. "He's what!?"

"Dead!" Taffy cried again. "Found him this morning. Dead as a doornail. Everyone heard what you said to him last night at the store. I don't know how you did it, dearie, but you sure fixed his little red wagon, didn't you?"

Chapter Eight

"ARE YOU *kidding* me?" The look of horror on Liza Jane's face must have tugged at the old man's heartstrings, or at least his conscience, because he had the decency to look embarrassed.

He also looked a little nervous. As Jimmy Dean began to explain what was wrong with Christabel, he took a few steps backwards, moving until his backside hit his messy desk. "Sorry ma'am, but the transmission ain't no good and has to be replaced," he said, subdued. He gave his cigarette a flick and Liza watched as it sailed through the air and landed dangerously close to a red plastic container that smelled of gasoline.

"But–," she stammered, trying to pull herself together. "Are you sure? It's going to cost me $1500?" She was still hoping she'd misunderstood him. It was possible, after all. Between his thick accent and the wad of chewing tobacco he'd kept tucked in his cheek before replacing it with the cigarette she'd only been able to understand half of what he'd said all day. At first she'd actually thought he was telling her she'd need to make a new "transition."

"Yep, and that's the lowest quote you're gonna get 'round here," he told her. "I'd barely be charging you for my labor at all."

Liza knew little about cars. She had no idea if that was a good deal or not. The only thing she knew about car salesmen and mechanics was that they were meant to be slimy lowlifes who liked to pretend to be sympathetic and your buddy while they took you for a ride.

She could at least put those fears to rest, though.

Liza let her eyes go glassy as she pulled herself out of her own mind she stretched the difference between them, until she reached into his thoughts and pressed. He flinched from the invasion and rubbed at his eyes, as though trying to get rid of a stray eyelash, but he'd have never known someone was invading his privacy like that.

Liza let herself be absorbed in the foreign mind of the old man for several seconds and then gently lifted herself out and snapped back like a rubber band. She'd seen and heard everything she needed. Jimmy Dean might have been a little scratchy and irritating, but he was telling her the truth.

Damn.

"Okay. Well. If you have to do it then I guess we have to do it. Just..." she paused and closed her eyes. It hurt–the thought of spending that much money on a car that was already ten-years-old. It hurt real bad. "Just let me go outside and think for a minute."

"Yep, go right ahead. I gotta make a call anyway," he shrugged. "Ain't like you're gonna take off and go nowhere."

There was an old metal bench next to an overflowing garbage can outside the shop. She sat down on the edge, keeping her feet far away from the brown patch of tobacco juice that had puddled on the ground.

She was lost in her own thoughts, bent over with her head buried in her hands, trying to tally up the costs and subtract it from the money she'd allotted herself for "incidentals" when the pick-up pulled up alongside of her.

"Hey, you okay?"

Even over what sounded like the death rattle of the truck, Liza recognized the friendly voice. When she looked up, she was met by the sunny, friendly smile of a Mr. Colt Bluevine. He was driving a dark blue Chevy with mud-caked tires and wore the same baseball cap. She was almost sure it was the same white T-shirt, too, unless he bought them in bulk and had one for every day of the week.

"You having a bad day?" he asked, this time with more concern. Liza was slightly embarrassed to have been caught looking depressed. She should've gone to the bathroom to do her deliberating.

"I've had better. You?"

He shrugged. "Just driving into town for some fertilizer. Seen you sitting here looking kinda lost. Can I help?"

"What's the fertilizer for?" she asked, curious.

"Dinner," he deadpanned.

Liza Jane's mood wasn't sour enough that she couldn't laugh at a joke.

"Seriously, though, it's for the trees," he smiled.

"What kind of trees?"

"Norway, white spruce, blue spruce. White pine...you know, Christmas trees. I'm a tree farmer, in a nutshell anyway," he replied.

"You grow Christmas trees?" she asked dreamily. She loved Christmas. She envisioned him out in the snow, cutting down a tree in his Carharrt jacket (she assumed he had one) and overalls. Walking down the side of the mountain with it balanced over his shoulder..."I love live trees."

"Yeah, well, you'll have to come out in a few weeks. I have a day where I bring in the horse and sleigh. I give rides around the farm, Mama and my sisters make hot chocolate for everyone, Santa comes for the kids...and you get to cut your own tree, of course."

Liza sighed. It sounded wonderful. "I'd like that a lot. Right now, though, I wouldn't have a way to get there."

"You got car trouble?" The concern on his face *looked* genuine enough.

"Yeah, a bit."

With one fluid movement he had his engine off and was out of his truck and standing in front of her. "What can I do to help?"

Liza was both flustered and a little embarrassed. She wasn't exactly a damsel in distress, after all. "Oh, nothing really. Just trying to figure out if I can really afford to spend $1500 on a new transmission."

"You talk to Jimmy Dean?" He gestured to the body shop window where they could both see the old man on the phone, gesturing wildly with his hands.

"Yeah," she answered. "He cut me as good of a deal as he could."

"Let me see what I can do. He's my uncle, Mama's brother. Might help."

He was already to the door and swinging it open before Liza could rise from the bench. "But–but," she stammered, jogging after him. "Shouldn't you at least take the keys from your ignition?"

Colt paused and looked back at his truck. "Why?" he asked at last, eyes raised. "Nobody would steal it. Everyone in town knows it's mine."

***

"Seriously, it is really nice of you to give me a ride home," Liza Jane said for the third time as they traveled down Main Street.

For a farmer, Colt's truck was surprisingly clean. It might have been covered in mud on the outside, but on the inside it was tidy, smelled good, and it even looked like he'd vacuumed recently. Her own car was a disaster area.

"Well, I couldn't leave you stranded there in town. We don't have but one motel in Kudzu Valley and it's the kind that rents by the hour. Unless, you know, you're wanting to earn a few extra bucks," he teased her, casting her a glance from the corner of his eye.

"Yeah, well, at the price I was going to have to pay for the transmission it wouldn't have been a bad idea."

"So I'll come by in the morning, around ten, and pick you up?" he asked.

Although Colt had not been able to bring his uncle down on the price, he *had* been able to talk him into doing a trade. As it turned out, Jimmy Dean also owned the used car lot next door. Liza had taken a look around with Colt and already picked out a few that didn't make her want to scream. She was attached to her car, but it was old and time for a new one. She knew it. And after being there for a while she'd already seen how necessary it was going to be to have a four wheel drive.

"Hey, I have a question for you," Liza asked abruptly. "I don't want to sound like I'm gossiping or anything but..."

"Shoot. What is it?"

"I ate at this restaurant, a buffet, and the waitress was really rude. Wouldn't even wait on me."

"Pregnant?" Colt asked.

"Yeah."

He nodded. "Athalie McClure. Kind of a whack job. I dated her for awhile in high school. Until she, uh, cheated on me. I guess you could say." He blushed, something Liza found endearing. "With a couple of different fellows. At the same time."

"Damn. That stinks. Don't know what she had against me. But yeah, I'll be ready in the morning. And I really appreciate you doing this," she said again.

"Well, I don't mind. Maybe you can repay me with dinner or something one night," he suggested casually.

She tried to ignore the wave of soft heat that passed between them and wondered if he could feel it as well.

"You wouldn't say that if you tasted my cooking," she chuckled. "It wouldn't be much of a repayment."

"Well maybe I wasn't talking about *you*," he retorted. "I was talking about me cooking you dinner. Sometimes I don't like eating alone. Company would be a nice repayment."

"You cook?" she asked with surprise.

"Yep. I have three sisters and a mama and not a one of them would let me out on my own without at least knowing how to make a decent pot of chili and spaghetti."

She could see it then, a country kitchen full of teenagers. A middle-aged woman standing over a boiling pot while three girls piled around the table, rolling dough. And a teenage boy, Colt she assumed, stirring something in a bowl. There was music coming from a radio, something fast with a lot of fiddles, and it mixed nicely with the comfortable sounds of chattering and laughter.

It was a scene she found herself wanting to step in and join very much.

"So what do your sisters do?" she asked.

"Well, Filly is a junior in college. She's a cheerleader," Colt answered. "Mare is a realtor over in Pinkham County and Bridle was a school teacher. She's not working at the moment."

"Wait," Liza said, trying to suppress laughter. "Your sisters are Bridle, Mare, and Filly? And you're—"

"I know, I know," he sighed with a grin. "We're all named after horses. Mama does love to ride."

"What's her name?"

Colt paused before answering, "Whinny."

Chapter Nine

IN A blind panic, Liza woke up with a start, sweat dripping from her forehead and pooling on the blankets around her. She'd had a terrible nightmare but couldn't recall a single thing from it. Now, wide awake and watching her digital alarm clock flash 3:15 am repeatedly into the darkness she found herself shaking, unnerved. What was that sound?

Whatever it was, it was chilling her to the bone. It was something she didn't think she'd ever heard before, something that made her skin crawl. Should she get up, light some candles? Sprinkle salt around her bedroom door? Light some sage?

And then it hit her, what the sound was.

It was silence.

There was nothing in the room other than the sound of her own ragged breathing.

Liza pounced out of bed and threw on the overhead light, instantly flooding the room with a rude fluorescent yellow. The faint hum from the old fixture settled her nerves somewhat and she could feel herself start to relax as she stumbled to the door and snatched her bathrobe down from the peg on the back.

"What the hell is the matter with me?" she demanded of herself. "What am I doing? I've never run a business before. I've never lived in the country before. What if I want Chinese in the middle of the night? What if I want Taco Bell? Who's going to deliver my pizza? How am I going to make friends? I don't know anyone. I don't go to church. I don't have kids to make playdates with other parents. Oh God, what if I have kids and I still haven't made friends and then they grow up to be crazy loner psychopaths and shoot up a school or something?"

She paced back and forth, her anxiety and panic leaving little tufts of smoke behind her with every step. She didn't realize it, but all the downstairs lights were now flickering off and on, unsettled by the nervous energy she was transmitting above them.

"What if I die here in the house? What if I have a carbon monoxide leak and die and nobody even knows that I am gone and I stink up the whole house and my body starts to rot and..."

The water in the bathroom sink began trickling from the faucet, followed shortly by the water in the tub.

"What if my business tanks and I don't make any money and I have to go on Food Stamps or–oh my God!" She paused in her pacing and looked at her reflection in the dresser mirror in horror. "I'm getting divorced! I won't have insurance anymore. How will I go to the doctor? What if I get sick?!"

The toilet flushed in response.

Had an outsider chosen that moment to approach the house they would've assumed someone was throwing a big old party. The lights flickered off and on like a fun house, the radio player in the living room cheerfully scanned through all the stations, playing several seconds of random tunes before going on to the next one, and Nana Bud's prized collection of Thomas

Kincaid music boxes all wound themselves up and began playing in off-tune unison.

Liza Jane heard and saw none of this. She was too busy having a breakdown.

In danger of leaving a permanent groove in her pine floors from the frantic pacing, Liza only stopped when her phone rang, the shrill song indicating her sister. She paused, cast it a furtive glance, and promptly ignored it.

Bryar Rose had some tricks of her own, however. When her voice should have gone to voicemail, it rang out through the room.

"Liza Jane Merriweather Higginbotham! You stop it!"

Now Liza really *did* stop. So did the rest of the ruckus. She would never even know anything happened downstairs. The lights gave one last halfhearted flicker and then the room went dark. The radio cut the Rolling Stones off mid-song, leaving the living room feeling oddly lonesome. Except for one light house music box whose faint strands of the "Love Story" theme wouldn't quite give it up, the living room was quiet.

The smoke that trailed her dissipated.

"Oh, for crying out loud," she muttered, marching over to where her phone was charging on her dresser.

"Hello?" she answered with irritation. "I was in the middle of a perfectly good rant and pity party. What do *you* want?"

"You were in the middle of waking up the entire east coast and causing a major power outage," Bryar complained. "You woke me up from the middle of a perfectly good dream that involved George Clooney and the little psychiatrist from *Law and Order: SVU*."

"I can't believe you still have a thing for Dr. Huang," Liza mused, dropping to the floor and leaning back against the dresser.

"Missing the point, sister," Bryar snorted. "Now what's the matter with you?"

Liza sighed. "Feeling overwhelmed. I don't know this town, I don't know these people. I don't know what I am doing. I–"

"Don't say it!"

"I miss Mode."

Liza could feel the burst of hot air that came from her sister's mouth, as hot and powerful as any dragon's. "Oh for crying out loud. You don't miss him. You miss the security of knowing what was going to happen every day. The stability."

"Yeah, maybe," Liza conceded. "But I still don't know what the hell I am doing here."

"You'll get to know the town," Bryar lectured her. "Mom didn't know the Boston area when she first moved there. Look at her now, she even has an accent."

"I think that accent is fake."

"Well, you know what I mean. You'll learn to fit in. You'll learn what it's about. And you're already meeting people. Like the Christmas tree farmer? He's been over there all the time helping you out. Probably done more for you in a month than your husband did in years."

"How do *you* know?" Liza demanded.

"I know stuff," Bryar replied airily. "So go back to sleep and keep it quiet. *Some* of us have stuff to do in the morning."

With that, the phone went dead.

Liza remained on the floor and considered her sister's words. Bryar was right. Liza *would* make friends and meet other people and learn the town and county. Like most everything else, though, she'd jumped right into the move and change without giving it any real thought. It was natural that she'd be nervous. She'd never lived in the country before; her suburban home up north had done nothing to prepare her for the life she was living now.

She'd be fine. And, if not, at least there was another witch in her corner who had her back.

***

"I didn't realize how dependent I was on the Internet," Liza said over the hum of the truck's engine.

"Yeah, I finally had to break down and get that out at the farm," Colt admitted. "That and a credit card machine. Nobody wants to carry cash anymore and I got tired of checks bouncing."

It was the third time she'd met him but now Liza Jane was feeling awkward. Damn her mother for putting ideas in her head.

"Sorry to be keeping you away from business like this," she apologized after a few minutes of awkward silence passed.

Colt raced over a pothole, sending both of them bouncing up in the air.

"It's no problem. Busy season is just now kicking up," he shrugged. "I had some errands to run in town anyway so it's okay."

Liza couldn't wait to get the vehicle sorted out so that she could start loading up supplies and bringing them into town. She also needed to go ahead and buy some paint and talk to someone about hiring a contractor. Again.

"Hey, you know anyone who can build stuff?" she asked. "I need someone who can work on my buildings. Pull up some carpet, build me some shelves and a countertop, and put me up some walls so that I can have an office."

"My cousin, Corn," Colt nodded. "He can do that for you. And he's a licensed electrician too."

"Um, excuse me, but *Corn*?" Liza asked incredulously.

"Well, it's short for 'Cornbread,'" he conceded.

"Your aunt and uncle named their child Cornbread?" she was still shocked. What was *wrong* with these people?

Colt laughed. "That's just his nickname. Nobody's called him his real name since we was kids."

"I think I'll have to go with his real name. I don't think I can go around calling someone '*Corn*,'" Liza shook her head.

"Okay, but his real name's Fartel..."

"Oh." She thought she might give "Corn" a try.

***

"It's a good truck," Colt assured her. "It's reliable. You'll get at least two or three good years out of it and that's about all you can ask for these days in a used vehicle.

Liza was still slightly embarrassed that he had stayed with her all morning while she'd looked around and test driven the vehicles she liked. She wasn't used to strangers going out of their way to be helpful and it was making her nervous. There was enough small town, mountain blood in her to accept his overtures politely and with grace. But there was enough big city paranoia in her to make her slightly afraid he might just be getting her in *his* good graces so that he could take her to some rural backroad and attack her.

The line was blurry.

In the meantime, she appreciated his expertise when it came to knowing cars (or trucks as the matter may be) and his family connections.

"If you say the Chevy is a good buy then I'll go with it," she said, hopping from the cab.

"You want to take it to a mechanic and have them look at it or anything?" he asked.

Liza snorted. "Well, I've been in town for less than a week and you and Jimmy Dean here are the only people I've met so far. The idea of having to find another mechanic is stressing me the hell out. I'll take your word for it."

Colt waited for her and chatted with Jimmy Dean while Liza went over all the paperwork and signed what she felt like was her past away. She'd had a lot of good memories in that Malibu. It was the only vehicle she'd ever bought brand new. It had taken her and her girlfriends for nights out on the town in Boston, had taken her and Mode up to Vermont for weekends away on more than one occasion...had brought her down to Kentucky to start a new life. She was attached to its stale interior, littered floors, and the sticky dashboard (a Coke can exploded in the car two summers ago when the temperatures soared above 90 degrees; she'd never been able to get it all completely off).

"So what made you go with the Chevy over the Ford in the end?" Jimmy Dean asked with interest.

Liza cringed as she watched him pick up a Coke can and spit into it, although she had to admit she was slightly impressed at the way he was able to get the whole wad into the small hole without hardly glancing at it. Practice, she guessed.

"Hmmm?" she asked, distracted by the line of tobacco juice that was running down his chin.

"The truck? What made you go with the Chevy? Was it the newer model, lower price...?"

The brown line of spittle wasn't moving. It was simply sinking into his grizzled skin, becoming a part of him. "It was red," she murmured, fascinated.

"Huh?" he asked, scratching his tuft of gray hair.

Colt snorted. "Don't ask. I have three sisters, remember?"

Once she'd moved everything from her old Malibu over to the truck and patted her car goodbye she turned to Colt. "Thanks for helping a lady out. I think I can handle it from here."

He reached out and patted her on the arm. The spark of electricity shot between them again, this time followed by a tuft of blue smoke that neither one of them could miss.

"Huh," Colt said, confused. "I must be holding onto static or something."

"Or something," Liza agreed, smiling faintly. Her whole body was buzzing like she'd been plugged into the wall and turned on "high."

"I think you probably could've managed this on your own, though," he said, his eyes twinkling.

Liza Jane might have swooned a little, but it could just as well have been the fact that she hadn't eaten yet.

"Oh yeah?"

He nodded and stuck his hands in his back pocket. "I'm keeping my eyes on you. There's something about you I haven't figured out yet."

As he turned to walk away she found herself studying his backside and the way his soft, faded jeans clung to him. "And I'm keeping my eyes on you, too," she said.

Colt stopped and turned. "I'm sorry, did you say something?"

Liza Jane flushed under his gaze. She didn't think she'd actually said that out loud. "Sorry, I just asked if your cousin was named after the country singer or..."

Colt threw his head back and laughed. "Oh no. His name isn't 'Jimmy Dean' at all. It's Sausagea."

"Of course," Liza said drily as she unlocked the door to her new truck.

Of course it was.

Chapter Ten

LIZA JANE HAD never owned a truck before and didn't know anyone who had except for her grandfather when she was little.

Now that she was riding high on the road, she wasn't sure how she'd lived so long without one.

After her second trip to The Healing Hands, Liza realized that she had nothing else left to bring. She'd been able to bring all the new stuff she'd ordered in just two loads—something it took her car at least four or five trips to accomplish the last time.

"Yeah baby," she sang as she hopped from the bed and landed on the pavement, a box full of office supplies balanced on her hip. Her boots, which she'd bought for aesthetic reasons but was finding them helpful for a variety of reasons when it came to living in the country, clicked when she walked.

She enjoyed the sound; it made her feel authoritative.

It had taken Colt's cousin, Cornbread "Corn" Crusher, only a week to do the work—*much* faster than she'd expected and quicker than it had taken the other group of guys the first time.

Of course, Corn had brought three men with him, which was probably a good thing because Cornbread was fond of his numerous "breaks" which could stretch into all afternoon.

Once, in the middle of installing the new floors, he'd stood up with his hammer mid swing, announced that he was going to walk over to the gas station to get a fresh cup of coffee, and left—hammer still in hand.

He hadn't returned by the next morning.

"Uh, guys?" Liza had nervously asked when the other men filed in and began picking up paint brushes to work on the wall in her treatment room. "Your boss gonna come back any time soon?"

"Don't know," the youngest of the three shrugged, his back to her.

None of them appeared to be particularly concerned regarding their boss' absence.

"Might do," another one had replied, his voice muffled by the fact that he had to talk around the e-cig that was permanently glued to the corner of his mouth. "Might not."

Liza could feel the heat rising in her neck, something between irritation and blind panic. She *had* to open the business soon. She couldn't go long without any income. Even if she tanked, she *had* to at least get the ball rolling again and try.

"Well," she attempted to sort it out again, although it was clear none of the men were going to be chatty, "will you all be able to work without him here?"

"We's workin' now ain't we?" the heavyset one they all called "Joker" answered. (She had no idea if that was his real name or not.)

Agitated at their lack of communication and Corn's abrupt departure, she'd stalked off to the second floor to stare at her boxes and panic in solitude.

There wasn't much she could do until the floors were in and she could get the furniture back out, but she liked looking at the boxes and rearranging their contents. Seeing all her supplies and products again sent a little thrill through her. It would be the first time in what felt like forever that she'd be contributing to her own living expenses and taking care of herself.

If she could ever get started.

Her internet had been installed, both at the house and at the store, and she tried getting online and setting up some social media pages for marketing. So far, the only people she knew in Kudzu Valley were Colt, Effie Trilby, Taffy, and her neighbor Jessie, so her local contact list was slim. Still, she'd never played around with the business side of social networking and she needed to learn. There was a lot to get done in a short amount of time.

That day, however, wasn't the day.

"Colt," she found herself moaning girlishly into the phone. "I hate to bother you but…"

"Hey, what's up?"

He always sounded so damn *cheery*.

"It's your cousin. He left yesterday to supposedly get coffee, and he's not back yet. I haven't heard from him and I'm getting nervous."

The sound of a motor on the other end of the phone was making it difficult for her to hear what Colt was saying in return.

"Sorry, what?!" she raised her voice and called into the receiver. "You're going to have to speak up a little."

The motor died down and she could hear Colt shuffling around with something. "Sorry," he replied. "Leaf blower. I asked if you were having trouble with the other men. They still working and all?"

Liza told him they were and then felt silly. She'd called him, *again*, and like a damn irritating woman who couldn't hack it on her own had interrupted his work. Worse, there really hadn't been a good reason to do it. The others *were* working, after all, and there was no reason for her to think her business wouldn't open on time, unless it was because of something she, herself, had screwed up.

And it wasn't like Colt was his cousin's keeper.

"Look," she apologized, embarrassed and appalled by her actions. "I feel stupid for calling. I shouldn't have bothered you. I know you're trying to run a business and with Christmas in just a few weeks you've got to be busy to your eyeballs. I'm just real anxious to get this open and I'm nervous about wanting it to do well. I guess I'm wound up pretty tight."

"No need to apologize; I know how it is, especially in the beginning. I can pretty much guarantee you, though," Colt returned smoothly. "I run a business myself. But, uh, don't worry none about the other part. Cornbread will be back tomorrow, next day at the latest. I guaran-damn-tee it."

An image flashed in Liza Jane's mind just then, something that crossed through the wires and space between her and Colt. The visual, of Corn in a narrow cot surrounded by a powerfully raw stench, made no sense whatsoever.

"Is everything okay? I mean, is he–"

"He's alright, just in jail," Colt laughed. "But it's okay. He has to go in every weekend between now and the end of December. He was probably too embarrassed to tell you yesterday; that's why he left the way he did. They'll let him loose tomorrow night. Knowing him, he'll probably head over to your place and catch up on his work even if you're not there so don't worry none."

Now the sound of the heavy sliding doors banging shut and the visual of the metal toilet and sink that had flashed through her mind earlier that morning made sense. Not that it was any less weird.

"If it's okay, can I ask what he got arrested for?" she asked with some hesitation.

"Oh yeah, it was drug charges," Colt answered. "Some opioids that weren't his. Found 'em when they did one of those traffic stops. They thought he looked high so they checked his truck and found the loose pills rolling around in the floorboard."

"Did he steal them or something?" she asked.

"Naw, not Cornbread. They weren't his, they were his buddy's. Guy admitted it. He was so stoned when he left Cornbread the last time he hadn't noticed them falling outta his pants pocket. Had a hole in it."

"Then why'd he get arrested?"

"Oh," Colt laughed. "Well, they might not have been his pills, but he was still drunk."

***

More freezing rain fell, making Liza even gladder she'd bought a four-wheel drive. Colt had been right about that. Driving on her snow-covered driveway when the time came would've been near impossible in her old car.

Liza wasn't a stranger to driving on the snow and ice, but driving in the mountains was a lot different from driving on snow-plowed city streets. She had to be careful not to go off the road and wind up over the cliff.

Now, as she cautiously made her way through the impending darkness towards home, John Mellencamp sang softly; "Little Pink Houses" scratched through the speakers.

At the top of the ridge, before she continued on towards her house, in an attempt to calm her nerves and forget the stress of what she was going through, she stopped and admired the scene before her. Ice was starting to cling to the tree tops and blanketed the ground like a layer of her Nana Bud's thick molasses, glossy and heavy.

A family of deer stood off in the distance; they watched her warily but seemed to sense that she didn't impose any threat to them. *She* wasn't going to shoot them so they remained where they were, cautiously nibbling at the ground.

Way down in the middle of the rolling hills she could see her house. From where she sat in her truck, and with the cozy front porch light sending out a welcoming beacon, it didn't look neglected and forlorn—it looked as regal and solid as the day her great, great grandfather had built it.

For better or worse, she was home.

Chapter Eleven

THERE WAS ONLY one way Liza could be absolutely certain who it was behind the crime. She was going to have to get down and dirty at her altar.

Although she was already *pretty* sure, she needed to be *positive*. If it wasn't Cotton, then it meant she still had an enemy out there.

Still wired and nervy from everything that had been going on lately, she first concentrated on calming herself down with a little meditation.

It didn't work.

Because she hadn't eaten since noon, when she tried to clear her mind all she could think of was dancing grilled cheeses and bowls of lobster bisque.

Instead of meditating, she stood and began jogging in place and flapping her arms up and down. Sometimes you just had to get the blood pumping.

Finally, with her wits about her, she sat down by her altar, bowl of water in her lap, and tried to relax again. It worked. Using a little rosemary sprinkled in for sight, she concentrated on the matter at hand.

Nothing happened at first. The heavy, labored sound of her breath filled the room and her own warmth lifted and wrapped itself around her (she always got hot doing spells, a witch's hot flash, if you will) but the water didn't move.

Liza was just about to give up when it began to shift at last. The tiny flakes of herbs began to dance in a circle, swirling around and around until they finally moved to one side and revealed a clear center.

And there, in the middle, was Cotton.

He was dead as a doornail, laying on the ground.

And then the vision disappeared.

***

"You going on another date?" Mabel Corrado (formerly Mabel Merriweather) pressed.

Liza Jane padded around the kitchen in her bare feet, the peeling linoleum cold on her soft skin. The whole kitchen needed a makeover. She'd have to do something about that.

"'Another' date Mom?" she laughed and rolled her eyes. "We haven't even been on a first one yet."

Liza was still shaken from the vision she'd seen the night before, not to mention everything else. She hadn't gotten very good sleep and wasn't particularly in the mood to deal with her mother.

"Oh honey, at your age you can't be picky about location and activity," Mabel warned her. "Just because he only took you through Hardees doesn't mean it wasn't a real date. You're a divorced woman. You have to accept what you can get."

"Mom! He was giving me a ride home and drove through Hardees because he wanted a coffee. He just asked if I wanted anything, too, and since I was hungry..." Liza let her voice trail off as she studied the contents of her refrigerator. It was a sorry sight.

"Well, if he's single and owns his own place then you'd better jump on this one right away." Mabel was a dog with a bone.

"I'm not ready to date. And besides, I'm not divorced yet. We're separated."

"Oh honey." Mabel's accusatory tone was replaced with one of pity, which was worse. "There's another woman's thongs in your dresser drawer and pink shaving razors in your bathtub. Trust me, you're divorced."

Though Liza Jane knew her mother was right, it still hurt to hear it.

"I'm about to come down there and drag you home myself after your little incident," Mabel continued. "What if you'd been there? What if you'd been hurt? I'm *sure* it was drugs."

"You're as bad as Bryar," Liza almost laughed. "What kind of drugs would I keep there?"

"I don't know," Mabel snapped. "Maybe people thought you sold the happy smokes or something. Those druggies get desperate. Maybe they thought they could smoke your candles."

"The candles are made from beeswax."

"Well, like I said. Druggies are desperate."

"Have you heard from Bryar? She called last night but I haven't been able to get back in touch with her."

Liza desperately wanted to talk to her sister, the only other person in the world who could understand how she felt about the ritual, but she wasn't picking up the phone. Liza had reached out to her with her thoughts and poked a little, but she didn't like to be intrusive. Besides, she hadn't received anything in return.

"Not a word," her mother sang. "But you know how flighty your sister is. Hey! Is that Colt of yours Whinny Bluevine's son by any chance?"

Liza headed to the living room. The house was freezing. Was she going to have to get someone to come out and see about the heat? Her grandparents had installed baseboard heaters but they'd all gone on strike at once—every last one of them, which she didn't think was possible. She needed firewood badly.

With a blanket wrapped around her she curled up on the couch. She knew she shouldn't, that it would sap her energy, but she couldn't help it. With steely concentration and a snap of her fingers the wood in the hearth before her jumped to life, the glorious flames immediately sending out waves of heat. Liza settled back into the cushions, tired but warm.

"Yes," she added at last. "That's his mother."

"See! He likes you. He's already talking about his mother."

Liza decided there was no point in telling her she'd been the one to bring it up.

"I went to school with her. She was a little odd," Mabel mused, "but I liked her. I think she was president of the FFA. Or 4-H. One of those clubs with a bunch of letters in it..."

Liza let her mother ramble on for a few more minutes before cutting her off.

"Sorry Mom, but I've got to get back over to the business. I've got to go get dressed."

"Okay honey, take care. And call people for that kind of thing, for Christ's sake. You're a lady! You don't need to be moving heavy things around by yourself."

"Yes Mommy," Liza replied and then belched loudly for effect.

"Well that was disgusting. Oh, and Liza! When it comes to your young man, don't be doing any of that hocus pocus around him. No shooting fire from your fingers or reading his mind or conjuring up the devil or anything," her mother sang with one last warning.

Liza hung up the phone shaking her head.

She'd *never* shot fire from her fingers, not once.

Chapter Twelve

LIZA WAS lining up her essential oils for the tenth time and changing the music on her CD player, opting for something Irish instead of the sounds of the relaxing waterfall she'd previously tried. It might have been peaceful, but it was putting her to sleep.

She hadn't slept much, thanks to nerves.

Since bringing in the new orders, and using her own sheets until the good ones arrived from Macy's, she was at least able to re-open, though it was on a more low-key basis than she would've liked.

Luckily, Colt's cousin Corn had been able to fix the things she couldn't. He'd done it all at cost.

She'd almost cried from his generosity.

In fact, everyone had been supportive and kind to her since the break-in. Even people she didn't know had gone out of their way, calling her with condolences, stopping in with casseroles and pies, and sending cards.

And yet, everyone in town still assumed she'd put a whammy on Cotton and killed him.

She *hadn't* killed him, she knew it. His body had been found in the woods, on the opposite side of the county. Time of death was estimated at a time when she'd been tucked in at home, making her fire roar (but not with her fingertips). She hadn't gone back out at all that night. She'd talked to her mother, emailed her sister, and vegged out in front of her fire, feeling sorry for herself.

But then there was the spell. She *had* seen his dead body. Had she killed him by mere *thought*? Had her words done it? Had she done something she wasn't aware of?

She wasn't sure.

When the tiny bell above her door jingled, Liza looked up, excitement coursing through her. Someone was there!

She was back in business.

"Please buy crap, please buy crap," she chanted softly as she left the treatment room and all but skipped to the front of the building.

Liza stopped dead in her tracks when she saw Colt Bluevine standing in the middle of her floor, looking lost with a bouquet of roses in one hand and a steaming Styrofoam cup of something in the other.

"You in the market for a foot rub?" she asked hopefully.

Colt grinned and stepped towards her, awkwardly holding out the bouquet. "These are for you. First day back and all. I thought they might be lucky."

Feeling nerves of another kind flooding through her, Liza brought the yellow bouquet to her face and sniffed them in appreciation.

For a moment she allowed herself to close her eyes and see him at the flower shop. She watched him mull through all of the pre-made flower arrangements, growing more and more overwhelmed and impatient at the choices.

"Would these be okay for a lady on her first day back at work after someone tried to sabotage her?" he asked the cashier helplessly, pointing at an arrangement of lilies.

"Probably not," the elderly woman smiled. "Those are for a funeral."

"Oh shit!" Colt blushed and snatched his hand back from the velvety leaves. "Then I'm gonna need some help."

Liza laughed and little and clutched the flowers to her chest more protectively.

"Did they say something funny?" Colt asked, scratching his head and nervously tugging on his cap.

"No," Liza replied. "I was just thinking of something that made me happy. Want to come in and sit down?"

She gestured to the settee but he looked down at it dubiously, like he was scared of the flowery pastel fabric and intricate cherry carvings. "Ummm…"

"It won't bite," she promised. "Almost all of the workers got past it unscathed."

"Almost?"

"Well, it stuck out and tripped Reggie but the stitches are coming out any day now."

Colt sent her a withering glance. "It's kind of girly."

"I *am* a girl."

"I might tear something on it," he warned her. "These are my work jeans."

"Oh here," she said, placing the roses down on the coffee table in front of the object in question. "I'll sit here and you take the chair over there. It's brown and has manly leather on it."

Looking much more comfortable, Colt lowered himself to the seat and then took in the rest of the room. "Looks nice," he offered. "Smells good in here, too. Heard the people in here before made a mess of it."

"Well," Liza responded, trying to remain diplomatic. "It did need a lot of work. And then there was the other mess, of course."

"I actually came today with an ulterior motive," Colt said, leaning forward and cracking his knuckles. He appeared to be full of nervous energy that morning and Liza found it endearing.

She was also once again struck by his good looks and the easy, confident way he carried himself. His fingernails were caked with grime and there were grease stains on his "work jeans." His baseball cap, advertising the hardware store in Kudzu Valley, looked as though it had never been washed.

And he smelled like a Christmas tree.

"What's your motive? Will it cost me money or get me arrested?" Liza teased him, feeling comfortable around him regardless of the fact she didn't really know him. Of course, so far he was her only friend in town if you didn't count her clients.

"Well," he scratched the back of his neck again and grinned. "Won't cost you any money but I can't guarantee the jail time. When you meet my sisters you'll understand."

"Huh?"

"My mama wants you to come over for dinner," he said, blushing. "Not just Mama. My sisters want you to come, too. They're just, you know, dying of curiosity and I haven't been giving them enough Intel, apparently."

Liza sat back, heart thudding. Did they think she and Colt were...?

"It's just that we don't get many new people moving in here," he explained. "You're the first in, oh I don't know, a couple of years I guess. We don't have a lot of entertainment, as you've undoubtedly noticed already. And you're already providing more than most."

Oh, so that was it, Liza thought, feeling a trifle disappointed. It was because she was new, because she'd brought drama–*not* because they thought he might be interested in her and they wanted to check her out.

"Well okay," she replied at last. "I would like to get out of the house. It's been a little lonely up there."

Liza could feel the relief radiating from him as he stood up and straightened his hat. "Well, how about Friday night then? About seven? Give you time to go home and do anything before coming out to the house?"

"That's fine," she agreed. "Where should I go?"

"My house is fine," he called over his shoulders as he headed to the door.

From her vantage point, Liza had the opportunity to study his backside. *Damn, it was fine.*

"You know where it is," he threw out over his shoulder. She could hear the grin in his voice. "We met when you were trespassing."

***

Morning business had been steady, thank goodness, and Liza was taking a much needed break when the door flew open. She looked up from her computer with a smile, expecting to see someone gratefully stepping in from the cold.

Instead, it was the sour-faced Detective Kroner.

Liza mentally applied a thick suit of protective armor around her exterior, something that would keep her emotions in check, and smiled politely at him. "Are you in the market for some relaxing foot scrub?" she asked brightly.

The Detective's face darkened and he scowled, taking in her business with a deep frown. "You sure got back in order fast," he declared, without a hint of kindness.

"I had a lot of help," Liza replied. "So what can I do for you?"

"I'm not sure you realize it, but the very man you accused of targeting you died the day *after* you accused him. And the day after *you* threatened to kill him."

"Yes, I know," she said evenly.

His eyebrows rose and a self-satisfied leer replaced the scowl. "You do know he's dead? And just how would you happen to have that information?"

"I imagine I have it the same way you know I threatened him in the gas station—by town gossip."

The leer faded.

"Besides, I didn't just randomly threaten to kill him," Liza pointed out. "I threatened to kill him if he did it again. Since he didn't do it again, I had no reason to cause his death."

"Be that as it may, care to tell me where you were the night of his death?"

"I was at home."

"Alone?"

Liza crossed her arms. "I live alone."

"Anyone vouch for your whereabouts?"

"I called my mother and talked to her and then emailed my sister a very long message. And then I conked out in front of my fireplace. That was my evening."

Detective Kroner snapped his notepad shut and stuffed it in his pocket. He would've looked much more commanding had he not had a mustard stain on his moustache. Liza could not take her eyes away from it. "Well ma'am, we don't take kindly to threats around here."

"And I don't take kindly to people breaking in and ruining my things," she snapped. "So I guess we're even."

"We *will* be talking again," he informed her as he marched to her door.

And then, just for the fun of it, she temporarily moved her door a few inches to the left as he reached it, causing him to ram into one of her windows.

She'd have to wash the mustard stain off the glass, but it had been totally worth it.

***

"Hellooooo!" a cheerful, female voice called from downstairs, her voice lifting through the floor and hitting Liza's ears just as she was leaning over to pick up a heavy box of aromatherapy candles. "Hello!?"

"Up here!" Liza called back. She stood, studied the box of candles, and considered the stairs. Take them now and not make it a wasted trip or come back for them later?

"I'm sorry but is anyone here?"

"Oh for....," Liza muttered as she picked up the heavy box, balanced it on her hip, and started down the narrow staircase.

The woman who stood at the bottom of the stairs was wearing a long blue jean skirt that nearly hit her ankles, appallingly yellow socks in sandals, a white buttoned-up top, and a deep blue cardigan that looked hand-knitted. Her long, deep brown hair swung down below her waist and from the split and uneven ends, didn't appear as though it had ever been cut.

She could've been thirty or sixty; her unlined, un-painted face made it hard to tell.

"Hi," Liza said, gently sitting the box on the floor. "I'm still kind of putting things together from where I just re-opened but I can probably still help you. Is there something you were looking for?"

The woman smiled courteously and folded her hands in front of her as though in prayer. "My, you *do* look just like your mama. And your granny, too. She was a good woman. You know, I was the one who let myself in her house after I got the call from the hospital and covered all the mirrors."

Liza nodded, trying to keep a respectful and interested expression on her face. She was still feeling tender and reminders of Nana Bud might just send her over the edge.

"Oh, I don't mean to get in your way," the other woman apologized. "There's just something I *have* to ask you about, something I hoped you could help me with. I'm Lola Ellen Pearson, by the way."

The look of helplessness on Lola's face had Liza's heart quickening. The poor woman appeared defeated.

"Well, sure," she found herself saying. "I have some chairs over here. Why don't you come and have a seat?"

Once they were seated, Liza leaned in closer. "So what's going on?"

"Well your granny, she…she sometimes helped me," Lola all but whispered. "Now I'm a good Christian and I don't believe in any of that devil's work but what your granny did was *God's* work, no matter what anyone said. She was a good Christian woman and was at church every Sunday. She led our choir!"

Liza nodded politely.

"But she did help me and I was hoping that you could, too," Lola continued. She bit her lip and looked down at the floor. "Now I don't gossip or nothing like that but I heard about Cotton. And what you done to him."

"Oh, but you see I didn't really…"

Lola smiled and waved Liza's words away. "What happened is between you and him and our dear Lord and Savior. I don't judge, only God and the little baby Jesus can do that. Besides, I never liked that Cotton no ways. He was one of them mouth breathers, you know what I mean? So annoying. So can you help me?"

"Well, I can try," Liza replied. "What, exactly, do you need?"

Lola straightened and primly smoothed down her long blue jean skirt. "It's about making someone pay for something bad that they did to me."

"You mean revenge?" Liza asked dubiously. She didn't really get into those kinds of spells. They could get messy. And sometimes they backfired. That was precisely why she hadn't done anything to Cotton, at least not intentionally.

A horrified look crossed Lola's face. "Oh no! I would NEVER seek revenge on anybody. I was just hoping that I could teach a lesson to someone who did something terrible to me."

Um, that would be revenge, Liza thought to herself but kept her mouth shut. Instead, she asked, "Can you tell me what happened and we'll kind of go from there?"

Lola leaned forward, her eyes glistening. "Well, it's *terrible*. The most horrible thing in the world, really. What they did is inexcusable, unforgivable."

A knot of fear formed in Liza's belly. Had someone killed a loved one? Not fixed her car properly and caused her to wreck? Stolen the family heirlooms?

"It was the Pizza Hut."

"Huh?" Liza wasn't sure she'd heard her correctly.

Lola nodded, satisfied with herself. "The Pizza Hut. Yep, it happened three weeks ago. We went the night before my big day, before my wedding to Hannelore Epperson? We went there for the rehearsal dinner. Spent $187, I'll have you know, and that was *with* coupons. It wasn't until later that night, after I got home and was reading my Bible, getting ready for bed, that it hit me."

Lola paused and tugged on her long, muddy brown hair. It fell like a waterfall to her lap, the split ends brushing her thighs.

"What hit you, Lola?"

"The diarrhear, that's what. All at once. Likely not have made it to the bathroom. Came all night, too. Awful cramps like you wouldn't believe. Called my sister and she brought me over some of that Imodium."

Liza might have laughed, if not for the fire flashing in Lola's eyes. "Well that sounds awful."

"Then the vomiting started. Oh, it just carried on all morning. My mama had her gallbladder out last fall and still had some of that Phenergan left over from the surgery so she brought it to me. It helped the vomiting, all right, but I had to hold onto my daddy walking down the aisle. Fell asleep in the car on the way to the reception at the Armory. We had to wait a full day before we could go on to our honeymoon to Gatlinburg! Lost $79.95 for that night because they wouldn't refund it."

Liza sat back, dazed. "So what is it that you need for me to do?"

"I want to make the Pizza Hut pay for what they did to me! They done gave me the food poisoning, is what. Made me sick because they used bad pepperonis. I knew they tasted funny," Lola snapped.

"Did anyone else at the rehearsal dinner get sick?"

"Naw, but I've always had a delicate stomach," Lola informed her.

"And you're sure it was the Pizza Hut? That it wasn't just one of those viruses?"

"I'm positive! And it was such a nice wedding, too," Lola said forlornly. "So much better than my wedding to Eugene, although our reception at the fairgrounds is something folks are still talking about, what with the salute to veterans we did during the ceremony. And, of course, Steryl and I eloped to Jellico so we didn't have much a wedding, just a Justice of the Peace. Maybe not as nice as my one to Buford but he worked for the railroad so he could afford that reception hall over in Richmond. We had real flowers, not fake ones, and bubbles for everyone to blow."

Liza sat back, dazed, as Lola Ellen Pearson ticked off her weddings, one by one.

"So can you help me? I would a gone to my preacher about this but we're Pentecostal and I feel like I've prayed enough. Had it up on the prayer board at church for two weeks but nothing's happened yet. Your granny was always helping me when the prayer circle wasn't enough."

"So you want to make the Pizza Hut pay for making you sick the night before your wedding?"

"Yes! You can do that, right?"

The hopeful look in Lola's eyes softened Liza just a little. She didn't normally like to perform hexes, but it would be bad to get started off on the wrong foot with what appeared to be the town gossip. Besides, she'd had food poisoning before. It wasn't nice.

"Okay," she said at last. "I can try. Now here's what you need to do..."

Chapter Thirteen

"YOU TRIED any Vic's?" Bryar demanded of her sister.

"Yes, *Mom*," Liza replied sarcastically before going into a dramatic coughing fit. She was pretty sure she'd cough up a lung if it went on any longer. "I've slathered so much on my chest that I am probably pickled for posterity at this point."

"What about a doctor?"

"I don't have one yet. No insurance. But I've made myself some chicken noodle soup and peppermint tea and–"

"You cooked?"

Liza could also see the incredulous look on her sister's face.

"Well, I *am* able to heat of a can of soup. I can't ruin that," Liza answered wryly. "I'm just upset that I just re-opened. I know it's Saturday but I hope I'm better by Monday. I don't want to be in there throwing up and sneezing all over clients."

"Probably a good way to ensure they don't return," Bryar agreed. "Well, let me know if I can do anything."

Liza knew *why* she was sick. It was the damned drafty house. She was bad about keeping the fire going all night, the heat only worked intermittently, and she couldn't find the feather duvets her grandmother had locked away. She'd found an electric blanket but was terrified of electrocuting herself. Not that there was an overwhelming amount of people who suffered death by electric blanket every year, but it wasn't something she could risk.

Her luck had not been great lately.

Holding a healing crystal in one hand and a steaming cup of tea in the other, Liza staggered to the living room in a ratty bathrobe she'd found in a closet. It smelled like her grandmother and mothballs.

She'd tried to keep the fire going but finally had to admit that she sucked at it. She could get the kindling lit without any trouble. It never seemed to "catch" the rest of the wood, though.

She kept resorting to magic.

"But I can't stay awake doing spells all night just to stay warm," she snapped.

When a knock came at her door she startled, a little jumpier than usual thanks to the Tylenol Cold and Flu she'd been taking, which was doing nothing for her nerves (or her cold or flu).

It was just the heating and air man, coming to check on her baseboard heaters.

"Thank God," she cried, almost throwing her arms around him. "It's freezing in here. I thought maybe I was doing something wrong."

Then she realized she was looking at Santa Claus. The repair man, a tall beefy guy in a thermal overall suit and steel-toed boots, had a long white curly beard, curly white hair, and little horn-rimmed glasses.

She watched in fascination as he bent over and tapped one of the units. "Cold as a witch's teats," he remarked cheerfully.

Liza grimaced a little and the man, whose nametag read "Whistle" flushed with embarrassment. "Sorry ma'am," he apologized. "Didn't mean no disrespect."

Liza laughed in spite of herself. "It's okay," she smiled. "*This* witch's 'teats' are frozen solid."

Now Whistle *really* flushed with embarrassment.

"Um, I hate to be rude or anything but you kind of remind me of..."

"Santa Claus?" he suggested, raising a bushy white eyebrow. "But I *am* Santa."

Liza looked at him, not knowing whether to laugh or not.

"Ho, ho, ho," he actually laughed, not managing to sound ironic at all. Instead, he sounded quite natural. "I'm town Santa but I am also a card carrying member of the International Organization of Santas."

To prove it, he whipped out a business card and handed it over. Liza studied his name, website, email, and little red, embossed sled in the upper right-hand corner.

"In fact, it's a good thing you called *now* because next weekend I'll be down in Gatlinburg, Tennessee for our annual

Santa conference. We do it every year, right before Christmas. It's a great time, but, I've got to tell you," he lowered his voice to a stage whisper, "some of those guys are really weird."

Liza had no doubt.

"And then, of course, our big day is just around the corner..."

Liza, nodded, eyes wide. *Okay, dude thinks he's Santa.*

She'd seen weirder. It wasn't like she was one to judge.

"So what you got it set on?" he asked as he rubbed his beefy hands together and looked around for the thermostat.

"It's on eighty right now," Liza replied. "I turned it up as high as it would go."

"Has it worked at all since you've been here?"

"A little," she replied hesitantly. She didn't exactly want to tell him that the only time over the past three days it had worked was when she used her mind to heat it up.

"Well, we'll have you sweatin' it up in no time. Let me go take a look-see around," he said.

Liza curled back up on the couch and wrapped an old afghan tightly around her shoulders. It was probably made by one of her relatives, the red and green colors the only thing she had out so far that were Christmassy at all. The warm mug of tea felt good in her hands and it was making her drowsy.

Liza must have drifted off for when Whistle re-entered the room and spoke her name she jumped straight up in the air, spilling her now-cold tea and sending the mug shattering to the ground.

The flames in the fireplace jumped accordingly.

"Um," Whistle began, as though trying to ignore what he'd just seen, "the good news is that it's not your unit, it's your thermostat. The bad news is they almost all of them need to be replaced, at least in the rooms you're going to be using. I have some out in the truck, but I'll have to charge you $50 for each one. Are there any rooms you'd like to be heating at the moment?"

Liza sighed, disgusted at the idea of having to spend more money she didn't have. "This room for sure, and maybe my bedroom and kitchen. My office. I guess that's all I need."

"You can hang blankets over the doors of the other rooms you can't shut off," he supplied helpfully. "We do that at home.

Just shut off the dining room completely during the winter. Eat dinner on the couch."

"Yeah, I can do that. It's just me," Liza sighed and then went off into a coughing spree.

"I'll just go get those thermostats," he said.

As he reached the door, however, he stopped and paused. "I know it's not my place to say this, but you don't look so good, Miss Liza. You're looking right sickly."

"Yeah," she threw him a wan smile. "I've seen better days."

"You got someone who can stop in here and check on you, bring you something if you need it?"

"Not yet," Liza replied brightly. "But I'll be okay. I've got my Vic's and my tea, and now I'll be warm."

Whistle did *not* look convinced. "Well, old Santa might just have some tricks up his sleeve yet."

Half an hour later, Liza had heat. In spite of her throbbing head and sore throat, she stood up and did a little dance in the middle of the living room floor, the rag rug sliding dangerously under her feet as she did her best "Risky Business" moves.

"Oh my God, thank you," she cried, wrapping her arms around Whistle's thick waist. He had the decency to redden, somehow managing to look even more like Santa, but appeared tickled all the same. "It's gonna feel so *good* in here!"

"And you need to build up your wood, too," he added as he started for the door. "I seen your wood pile and you're running low. This heat here ought a keep you warm the rest of the winter but you need that back-up heat, 'specially since you ain't got no generator if the power fails you. Which it's likely to do at some point. Last year we got an ice storm here that threw the whole town's power out for damn near three weeks."

"Yeah..." she began slowly. "Where *would* I get wood?"

Whistle cocked his head to the side and pointed out her front window. "Well, ordinarily, we'd just go right out there and cut some in the spring and let it age. But I'm guessing you didn't get to do that..."

"You'd be guessing right," she said. "And I don't have an axe or anything to do it now."

"Well, I know some landscapers who probably have some cut. I'll send 'em your way," he told her.

And, with that, she was left all alone again. She'd enjoyed her company, and really enjoyed the fact that the room was heating up. She'd been just as ecstatic when the internet guy had come out, at the thought of having someone else in her house, even if he was ten years younger than her and listened to Kanye West on his iPod the whole time he was there.

"So explain this to me again," she'd said as she'd towered over him, peering at the screen while he typed away.

"It's not broadband so you don't have unlimited downloads on it," he explained.

"Well, that's okay, I don't download a lot. Mostly just You Tube, social media, stuff like that."

The guy had grinned then and looked at her like she had two heads. "Well, those count as downloads. See, you have a limited, storage let's say. And every time you watch a video, look at a picture—whatever, it eats it up. You've got a month's supply here but if you watched ten videos it would all be eaten up in a day."

"You're kidding me," she gasped. "You mean to tell me I am paying almost $100 a month and I can't even watch stupid cat videos on You Tube?"

"Well, you can between 2 am and 7am. That's your bonus time."

Liza saw a lot of late nights in her future.

***

A few hours later and she was still enjoying her heat and sitting on the couch, flipping through her Book of Shadows. She'd started it when she was sixteen and, at two hundred pages, it was full of rituals she used, rituals she liked but would never get around to using, pretty pictures she'd clipped out of things, notes she'd taken after spells, experiences she'd had with things that were both good and bad, and little pieces of paper, leaves, and stuff she'd collected over the years....

"Oh my God," she looked up and rolled her eyes. "I am the Pinterest version of a witch. I will *never* get around to doing all of these things."

Liza was trying to find something technological to help her get more use from her internet when there came a knock on the door.

Liza looked down at her ratty pajama bottoms, *Freebird* T-shirt, and puppy dog slippers and grimaced. The dogs even barked when her feet hit the ground. She hadn't washed her hair or bathed in nearly four days. It had been too cold.

Before opening the door Liza stood, picked up a silk rose from an old flower arrangement on top of the console table, closed her eyes, and focused all her attention inwards. Lacking the time to make herself presentable, she instead focused on changing the perception of the person on the other side of the door.

"By the powers of the west, I take the beauty from this flower. With love and light I shine with its power. The beauty and grace is all they'll see, with harm to none, so mote it be," she chanted softly, feeling the spell slightly silly but necessary.

A surge of light and warmth washed over her in gentle waves, encompassing her like a Sherpa blanket.

The spell wasn't going to make her a beauty by any stretch of the imagination and if she looked in the mirror *she'd* still see the same disheveled hair, dark circles under the eyes, and fuzzy skin with the stray black hair that always wanted to poke out of her left cheek.

To others she'd just look a little tired. (Ordinarily Liza Jane was a very attractive woman, but it took a *lot* of Clinique on her bad days.)

It wasn't a *complete* fix, but it would work.

The matronly woman on the other side of the door was as round as a watermelon with hair that reminded Liza of the color of the squash her Nana Bud had grown. *This* woman's hair was short and curly and hung to her shoulders in Shirley Temple ringlets; her smile stretched from ear to ear. In her hands she carried three containers of Cool Whip.

"Hello there," she said cheerfully, not waiting for an invitation as she stepped into Liza's house and slammed the door behind her with her foot. "Chilly out there ain't it?"

Funny that. No matter where in the country you lived, the weather was always an acceptable, universal topic.

"A little," Liza answered slowly. She closed her eyes and saw the woman before her at home, bending over a table while she beat dough in her bare hands. Whistle stood off to the side, white hair sticking up all over his head, asking when supper was ready.

Whistle's wife, then, Liza knew.

"I'm Honey," the woman offered brightly. "I'd offer you my hand but it's full. You got someplace I could put these?" She used her head to nod towards the containers she carried.

"Um, in the kitchen?"

Honey followed Liza into the kitchen. Liza wasn't embarrassed to have anyone in the kitchen with her. It was clean enough, especially since Liza wasn't cooking much, although it was still a little bare since she hadn't gone on any recent supply runs.

"I'll just stick these in the fridge," Honey said, making herself at home. "Now the top one here is chicken noodle soup. It's homemade, my mommy's recipe. The bottom one is banana pudding. I made it this morning. It's Whistle's favorite. You're lucky there's any left. The one in the middle, the little 'un, it's some cat head biscuits. I'll leave them here on the counter."

"I thought they were all Cool Whip," Liza said, still confused by Honey's presence. And by what a "cat head" biscuit was.

"Oh Lordy, no," Honey laughed. "Just hillbilly Tupperware is all. When Whistle said you was sickly I *knew* I couldn't let you be up here by your little self, without nobody to take care of you. I said, 'Whistle, that poor little thing ain't got nobody in the whole wide world right now to love on her. I'm not gonna sit by and let that happen!' Now let's me and you go have us a good sit down."

Liza dutifully allowed Honey to lead her back to the living room where both women settled onto the couch.

"Lawd, it's good to be back here and see this old place lived in," Honey sighed as she began kicking off her boots and peeling off her gloves. She might have carried chicken noodle soup in Cool Whip containers but she carried a Dooney & Burke purse and her perfume was Chanel No. 5. "Sad to see a house not being a home, isn't it? Especially when it's meant to be. Lots of fond memories here."

"You knew my grandmother?"

"Oh darlin', *everyone* knew Rosebud. She was one of our most treasured members of the community. And oh, the dances she used to have here ever Christmas? Pushed that rug and couch back and Paine would bring out the fiddle. You never saw a place so alive with...*magic*."

Honey smiled at the memory and Liza herself almost teared up. She had never seen that herself. She'd missed so much. So much.

Honey, perhaps with a sixth sense of her own, changed the subject. "You ever seen that fairy house she made for the Garden Club?"

Liza shook her head no.

"It was downright magical. Jumped to life every time you looked at it, it did. Made it out of a tree stump with little mushroom chairs and fairy dolls. Go down to the Court House. It's still there. Your granny was a true artist." Honey smiled at the memory.

"I miss her," Liza said vehemently and was no longer surprised to feel the tears stinging her eyes and her nose swelling with pressure.

"Well *of course* you do, of course," Honey cried. She leaned over and took Liza's hand in her own and squeezed so hard Liza felt Honey's own spirit flow through her. She might not have known it herself, but Honey also had the magic inside. It was comforting. "Her and Paine? They was some of the best people I knew. We *all* thought the world of them. That's why we're all so glad you come here to take her place."

"Take her place? Oh, I couldn't do that," Liza said.

She'd *never* be her grandmother. Rosebud was a spitfire, full of life. She'd loved everyone without taking any crap from anybody, had been full of energy until the day she died. She'd been involved in every club and organization in the county, from the Women's Club to den mother for the Boy Scouts. She'd held dances right there in her own living room and had waltzed with her husband, right up until they were eighty.

Liza sometimes wasn't even sure she *liked* being around people all that much. Not all the time anyway, not like her grandmother had. "I'll never be like my grandmother."

Honey beamed, a secret smile playing at the corners of her mouth. "You felt a call to come here, didn't you? A pull that was more than just trying to get away from your unfortunate situation?"

Liza had to laugh at Mode, her ex-husband, referred to as her "unfortunate situation." But Honey was right; she *had* felt a "pull." "I guess I did," she replied, remembering the exhilaration shed felt at seeing the mountains as they'd grown nearer and nearer on her drive down. "But how–"

"You were *meant* to come, to take her place," Honey insisted.

"Oh but I–"

"You really *don't* understand, do you?" Honey slapped her hand on her knee in glee, her little ringlets swinging with her laughter. "We *know* what you did to Cotton Hashagen–"

"But I–" Liza protested.

"And we've heard about how you cured Taffy. We *know* you've come to take over from Rosebud, dear. You're our granny witch. And we're real glad to have you."

***

Liza stood on her ridge, she'd decided to name it "Mistletoe Ridge" thanks to the abundance of mistletoe clumps that hung precariously from all the treetops. She didn't think her grandparents would mind, though Bryar had laughed like a hyena.

"You're getting weird," she'd scoffed.

She didn't mind being weird. It beat some of the other things she'd been called over the years.

In the hazy fog she shivered, sneezed, and scrutinized at the basin with wonder. It was freezing and she could no longer feel her toes but something had woken her up from a deep, cold medicine-induced sleep and called her out there.

Since Liza never ignored those orders she'd slipped on heavy barn boots and a thick flannel jacket that had belonged to her grandfather and made her way to the ridge that overlooked the valley.

The sun wasn't even out yet. The sky, lost in a hazy silver, couldn't decide if it was day or night. The ground, covered in thick frost, looked unnatural–like someone had rolled a sheet of wax paper out over it.

It hadn't snowed yet, despite being close to Christmas. Liza hoped it would. She'd never *not* had a white Christmas. Each day the sky looked and smelled like it wanted to, but nothing happened, other than rain and sleet.

"You'll be sorry when it does," her mailman had warned her. "You'll be stuck here for days."

But Liza liked the snow. She enjoyed watching the puffs of cotton balls fall from the sky, the intricacies of the crystals, the sweetness of gathering it in a bowl and mixing it with milk and sugar...

Now, though, Liza hugged her arms in front of her chest and recalled another time she'd stood there, in that same place, although she'd been much younger then and the world had felt much farther away.

She hadn't been alone that time, either; that time she'd been with her grandmother. Even now she wasn't completely sure what had happened, but whatever it was made her feel safe–like maybe there *was* something bigger than her mother and Bryar Rose and maybe even bigger than her grandmother out there in the universe.

And now, standing in the silvery light watching the valley and remembering the feel of her grandmother's frail, yet powerful, body beside her Liza thought of the conversation she'd had with Mabel before returning to Kudzu Valley.

"I don't know *why* you'd want to throw your life away and move to that old place out in the middle of nowhere," Mabel had complained. "And right here before Thanksgiving, too! Are you out of your damned mind?"

Even now, as Liza immersed herself in the tobacco scent of her grandfather's jacket and stood mesmerized by the fog rolling over the ground in giant cotton candy puffs, she could *still* hear her mother's plaintive voice.

That was one of Liza's *other* gifts: everything that had ever been said to her was forever imprinted in her mind like the grooves of a record, something she could pull up and listen to whenever she wished—and more often than not, when she *didn't* wish.

She could see her now: Mabel Merriweather Corrado, glorious jet-black hair fanning her youthful face, cheeks flushed with annoyance, stomping around Liza's tiny rental unit in Beverly, complaining.

"*Gawd* Liza Jane, we moved out of that joke of a place to give you and your sister a better opportunity," she'd wailed. "A better life for the two of you!"

Actually, her mother had moved from Kudzu Valley because she'd met husband #2 at a Rite Aid convention in

Harrisburg, Pennsylvania. She was also there for the convention and they'd fallen in love (or something) over cold, rubbery banquet chicken at dinner on the first night. It hadn't taken him much to sweet talk her into marrying him and moving to the Boston suburb where he owned a townhome. Mabel had always been a bit of an opportunist and wasn't enjoying living back at her parents' house with two young children. She'd been looking for a way out of it *and* the town for awhile so the handsome stranger who appeared to be financially stable must have looked like a prince to her. And Mabel, with her movie-star looks, charming and witty personality, and sob story must have been a dream to him. He wasn't exactly putting notches on his bedpost at the time.

Liza's father had passed away in a freak lawnmower accident when she was a toddler. He hadn't been run over *by* the lawnmower or anything; it had fallen on his head. Why George McIntosh, owner of Johnson's Home Improvements and Hot Tubs, had thought hanging Cub Cadets from the ceiling was a good idea was beyond her. Freeman Merriweather had literally been in the wrong place at the wrong time. He'd had no idea that the

Maytag dryer, priced at a Black Friday special of $199, would be the last thing he'd see.

Gene Corrado was a tolerable man. When she was a teenager and going through her mean and vindictive stage, which she referred to as her "gaining independence" period, she'd told anyone who would listen that he had the personality of a slab of margarine.

Mabel had *not* found that amusing.

As an adult, Liza could grudgingly admit that he'd done his best to be a stepfather to two wild, obstinate mountain children he didn't understand and, in spite of the fact Mabel's parents were sure that with a surname like "Corrado" he must be mafia, he was a gentle soul.

Mabel was happy, too. (Maybe not as happy as Liza's grandparents had been when their daughter had moved out—there'd been a collective sigh of relief all around when *that* happened, but still...)

Mabel might not be living in the lap of luxury, but she was better off than most. She had a nice split-level home in an affluent neighborhood outside of Boston, a timeshare in a coveted Las

Vegas condo community, and a cappuccino machine she'd paid full price for (*not* one grabbed at 4:00 am as a Black Friday door buster as she liked to point out to her neighbors).

Mabel Merriweather Corrado had no love for her old hometown or the people who lived there and spoke of her former classmates back in Kudzu Valley with disdain.

"I got *out*," she'd brag to Liza Jane and Bryar Rose, jabbing her perfectly manicured finger in their chests. "Believe you me, you'll thank me one day that I got *you* girls out too. You'll be glad."

To be fair, Bryar Rose *was* glad. Bryar didn't remember her father or living in the town at all so she had no sentimentality for it. As a child she'd returned with Liza four times and only once as an adult and then again for their grandparents' funerals.

She'd driven down with Liza for Paine's funeral and at that time, Bryar had recoiled in disgust as they'd driven down Main Street and Broadway and regarded the tiny town like tourists, staring at the empty windows, quiet sidewalks, 10 Commandant signs stuck stoically in some of the yards (sometimes next to Confederate flags), and what appeared to be more than a dozen yellow-signed Dollar General Stores.

Bryar Rose didn't shop discount.

"Who would *live* here," she'd whispered during the graveside service as the attendees broke out in "The Old Rugged Cross" and the two women had pretended to mouth the words since they didn't know the lyrics. "Did you know you can't even *drink*?"

Liza had "shushed" her and rolled her eyes.

Bryar had stayed on for one more day, but that had been enough for her. Even though Liza was planning on remaining for a week to help her grandmother, Bryar had marched into the kitchen and announced with glee that she'd changed her plane ticket and would be leaving with their mother.

Mabel had looked visibly relieved that she'd had some influence on at least *one* daughter.

"Sorry LJ," she'd said and Liza thought she probably meant it. "I just can't. We're working on an album right now and I'm in the studio. And honestly, if I eat fast food or Pizza Hut one more time I'm gonna barf."

Their grandmother, sitting quietly in one of the old wooden chairs in the corner of the kitchen, her hands folded in her lap, had winced. She'd always prided herself on the "good country cookin'" she'd provided her family when they came to stay with her: the fried chicken, the mashed potatoes, the corn on the cob and macaroni and tomato juice...the apple stack cake.

But she hadn't been able to cook in weeks, not since her husband went to the hospital for the last time. Rosebud hadn't left his side, sleeping curled up next to his body on the thin, hard hospital bed.

Both girls had seen the guilt and sadness in her eyes at Bryar's words.

"Aw Gran." Bryar had rushed over to her then and, in a rare show of affection for the no-nonsense pop music producer, she'd taken her much smaller grandmother in her arms and held onto her while they both cried.

Bryar's bark had always been worse than her bite. And her gift was empathy. If she didn't block some of it out, she got it *all*.

Liza stopped remembering now and let her mind refocus. She knew she should've just stayed on then and not returned to Massachusetts. At that point she and Mode had only been married for a few years but they were already having problems that Liza knew were warning signs she shouldn't ignore.

Even Bryar, who only possessed a little glimmer of the sight, had known. "You can stay if you want," she offered hesitantly from the driver's seat of their rental, waiting for their mother to join her. "You don't *have* to go back at all. I'll go to your place and pack your stuff. Just leave his ass."

"Why would I do that?" Liza had asked in bewilderment. But she found the idea more tantalizing than she should have that early on and a spark was lit at that moment that would never truly extinguish.

"Whatever," Bryar had grumbled. "But seriously. At least promise me that while you're here you'll find better music. You can't join the locals and listen to this country crap. It's terrible!"

Now slightly offended, Liza eased back from the car and crossed her arms. "I *like* country."

"You don't even know what it is! You'd never listened to it until this week."

"I knew who some of them were," Liza insisted stubbornly. "I knew Garth Brooks. And I like this guy, Jason Aldean? And Blake Shelton? They're good songs."

"They're *not* good songs," Bryar had muttered under her breath but to Liza she'd rolled her eyes and cried, "Good Lord you're turning into one of them. The next thing I know you're going to be driving a big truck, wearing shorty shorts with your hiney sticking out, and tying your shirt at your bellybutton."

The image of a truck flashed behind her eyes and Liza had smiled at the idea, not finding it a bad one at all. Still, she had no idea what her sister was talking about. She hadn't seen a single person in Kudzu Valley who looked like that, although the truck part was certainly true.

But, she hadn't stayed. She'd left eight days later, leaving her grandmother to live alone in a house full of memories and maybe even ghosts. On her last night they'd walked outside at midnight and stood in the same place Liza stood now.

Together, they'd knelt on the ground and studied the moon. Then, together, they'd clasped hands, young and old, and lifted them high in the air and spoke to the faraway shimmering object as though it were a friend who could respond.

And maybe it *had* because, seconds later, the moon had grown twice as bright and a falling star had bolted through the sky almost right towards them and then disappeared over the mountain the people in Kudzu Valley called "Big Hill."

Liza had never seen another one since.

Chapter Fourteen

AT THE beginning of the day, Liza's soft gray, wool dress had been comfortable and warm. Her black leather boots had felt like butter on her feet, the spiked heels giving her an extra inch or two that made her preen. Her makeup, all her favorite shades from Clinique, was impeccable. Her hair was smartly straightened with the best straightener she could (okay, her ex-husband could) afford for Christmas, and her silky underwear felt heavenly against her skin.

By closing time she was a hot, tired, itchy mess with sweat stains under her arms and frazzled hair. Her mascara was clumping on the top and running on the bottom and her plumb-colored lipstick stained her top row of teeth. She had a wedgie from hell and her bra straps kept sliding down her arms.

And her feet were *killing* her.

"I will not wear tennis shoes. I will not wear orthopedic shoes," she swore as she leaned back on the settee, one of the few things that hadn't been destroyed, and rubbed a balm onto her toes and then sighed with audible relief.

She didn't care how ridiculous she might look or how uncomfortable it might get; she would *not* give her up her favorite clothes. She still loved her jeans, but only when paired with the right accessories: a great necklace, a scarf, some fabulous cowboy boots, bangles...

She was vain; she couldn't help it.

When the door chimed, the two women who entered were met by a scene that made both of them snicker. Liza, skirt hiked up to her thighs; bare leg stuck out in front of her while she rubbed bright blue cream on her toes, moaned in relief.

"Oh my God," Liza cried when the women closed the door behind them and walked towards her. "I am sooo sorry. Usually, I hear someone before they come in and..."

She quickly stood and pulled her dress down, modestly covering her legs. She hadn't even shaved in two weeks. There was no telling what they'd seen. Embarrassed, she searched for her sock and boot, both of which had gotten pushed under the settee.

The older of the two women, a striking brunette in dark brown pants and a red wool coat with a rhinestone Christmas tree pin on the lapel, laughed. "Honey, we've *all* been there."

The younger, a pretty little redhead in a beautiful cream-colored coat and brown riding boots that appeared *not* to be hurting her feet, nodded. "For me? Every day. The first thing I do when I get home is kick my shoes off and stick my feet in a paraffin bath."

"Yeah, well, at least *you* wait until you get home," Liza grumbled.

She wondered if it would be worth it to make the ladies forget what they'd seen but ultimately decided against it. She had to pick her battles. And it wasn't like she had warts on her toes or anything.

"So is there anything I can help you ladies with today?" she asked instead.

The older one had already started wandering around the store section, picking up bottles and boxes and studying the backs before placing them neatly back on the shelves. There was something familiar about her, but Liza couldn't quite put her finger on it.

"You make your own soaps and lotions?" she called out to Liza over her shoulder.

"Well, I *do*, but I didn't make those. They're still homemade, though. I order them from a lady up in Massachusetts. I hope to have some of my own in here soon," Liza said.

And she fully intended on making her own soon. Very soon. She was just so tired. Every night she just wanted to go home and pass out on the couch. Maybe eat some ice cream or something else that she could consume right out of the carton.

"I like these candles," the younger one said as she picked up a cinnamon holder and gave it a sniff. "I make my own candles. Not to sell or anything, just to put around the house. I like crafting."

"She's not giving herself enough credit. Her candles are beautiful. She buys antique teacups and other interesting containers from flea markets and yard sales and uses them as her containers," the other woman called. She'd moved on to Liza's facial products—her lip balms, mascaras, and makeup removers.

"I'm Liza, by the way." Now that she had her shoes on, she could join the women who were now wandering around her business, taking in everything they could. "I'd offer to shake your hand but, well, you just saw it on my feet so..."

"I'm Mare," the younger one said. "And that's my mother, Whinny."

Liza could now see the resemblance between Colt and his sister. Her hair was redder than his, and her skin not as dark from working out in the sun, but they both had the same lively eyes, strong jawlines, and full lips.

"You're Colt's family," Liza replied, feeling even more embarrassed by her own appearance. "It's nice to meet you. He's been very helpful to me since I came to town."

"That's my brother," Mare agreed. "He'll help just about anyone."

Liza's heart sank a bit at that. It wasn't like she was *interested* in him, but it somehow made her feel less special, and that didn't feel nice.

Whinny strode over to where Liza stood by the counter and studied her. She must have noticed and recognized the look on Liza's face because she sent her daughter a withering glance. Placing a light hand on Liza's arm, she said, "We've heard *a lot* about you. Frankly, I am glad to see that your lipstick bleeds and that *you* can't wear those ridiculous shoes without getting blisters like the rest of us. I was beginning to think you were a saint."

Liza, a little tickled that they'd "heard a lot about" her, and grateful for the other woman's words, smiled with foolish delight. "Well, the cream *does* make them disappear very quickly. So that helps."

"She's good, Mom," Mare shouted from the treatment room. "She's even trying to make a sale!"

"I wanted to thank you for the dinner invitation. I look forward to it. I've been eating out almost every day or getting microwavable stuff," Liza admitted. "You know, it's very hard to grocery shop for one person. It feels so wasteful. I made myself a pot of macaroni and cheese the other night and after two bowls threw most of it out. Well, I actually fed it to a dog that's taken up with me. I don't know where he came from. Or if he is really a *he*."

Whinny nodded, a touch of sadness in her eyes. "I know you what mean. My husband passed away and with all my kids out of the house I rarely cook the way I used to. It's not only wasteful but a little sad sitting at a big table all alone."

Liza, thinking the same thing about eating at her grandparents' table, agreed. Something passed between the two women then and Liza understood that she'd made a friend, though she wasn't sure quite how. It had been a long time since she'd had a female friend other than her sister.

"So, do you have any potions or anything for sale?" Mare asked as she all but skipped back over, appearing satisfied that she'd scrutinized everything on Liza's shelves.

Liza, taken aback, was at a loss. "*Potions?*"

"You know, love spells, getting younger, stuff like that," Mare prodded, giving Liza a little nudge.

Whinny rolled her eyes and swatted her daughter with her little Kate Spade purse. "Forgive my daughter. She watches a lot of television and has seen *The Craft* one too many times. Mare, please."

"People say you're really good at the massages and stuff," Mare said with a sulk. "And then what you did to Cotton. I just kind of hoped that maybe you had some fun things to, I don't know, bring in the men or something."

"I think you do just fine bringing in the men, dear," her mother muttered.

"I don't know what you think about Cotton but I didn't–"

"But people said that you yelled at him in the store and..." Mare's voice dropped off when she caught her mother's strong glare.

"I saw him outside one night. He was lurking," Liza explained, feeling faintly embarrassed. "And then my store was trashed. The detective laughed it off."

"Yeah, cuz they're cousins," Mare spat.

"Well, that part is true enough," Whinny agreed.

"But I didn't do anything to him. I honestly don't know what happened," Liza continued.

"But can't you do a spell and see and…" Again, Mare let her words end without finishing her thoughts.

"So did everyone know that my grandmother…"

Mare nodded. "Oh yeah. But she wasn't, like, freaky or anything. She was always real classy about what she did. I hoped, you know, that since you're young you might…"

Mare stopped and had the decency to look humiliated.

"It's okay," Liza assured her. "I try to help when I can but I'm afraid I'm probably not as exciting as you might think. Most of what I do are small things. Little things to help people, to heal them."

Mare and Whinny exchanged glances then that Liza couldn't quite interpret. Sometimes, the magic between a mother and a daughter was too much for even a seasoned witch to cut through.

But then Whinny laughed, a merry sound that broke the ice, and tugged on her daughter's hair. "Why don't you get to *know* her before you start asking her for love charms?"

"Yeah, sorry about that," Mare apologized.

The women chatted with Liza for several more minutes and then excused themselves, citing the need to get home before it got too dark.

"We'll see you in a few days," Mare said. In her hand she carried a mint green bag full of various creams, guilt purchases for being rude but Liza didn't mind. She did, after all, have bills to pay.

She'd take what she could get.

When the door closed behind them, Liza leaned back against her counter and laughed. Her last date with anyone other than her ex-husband had been fourteen years ago.

Still, she watched a lot of movies and was fully aware of what had just happened: she'd just been checked out by a man's family.

***

"I'd advise you to get yourself an attorney, ma'am."

That's what Detective Kroner had told her over the phone, minutes after she opened her business the next morning.

Cotton Hashagen's cause of death was ruled "undetermined." They couldn't figure out *how* he died, Kroner and apparently half the justice department in Kudzu Valley just knew *Liza* had something to do with it.

Cotton Hashagen had been discovered in the woods, one shoe off, glasses gone, and neither found anywhere near him. He'd died from internal bleeding but had no significant marks on his body other than a bruise on his head that didn't look large enough to cause such an issue.

"Probably runned into a door or somethin'," an officer said while he poked around Liza's business. "Cotton drunk a lot. He could a done it that way."

Detective Kroner had *not* been pleased with that little slip of information.

And Liza Jane Higginbotham was being blamed for *it*. Whatever *it* was.

An attorney. *How* was she supposed to find one of those, or pay for one? She had budgeted just enough money to get her through the toughest times of the year. A criminal defense attorney, if it came to that, could cost a fortune. And she had no alibi. Nothing.

Of course, the only "evidence" they had was the fact that she'd accused him of breaking into her business and had then yelled at him in public.

And that she was a witch.

She *knew* she hadn't killed Cotton.

(Okay, she was almost certain she hadn't killed him.)

But how could she prove it?

"And you tried looking into it?" Bryar asked her for the millionth time.

Liza, pacing up and down the stairs at work, trying to get the blood pumping before she let loose and did something stupid, like make that Detective Kroner fly through the air and wrap himself around the town's only caution light, sighed. "Yes! Twice now. I can't see a darn thing, other than that it looks like I *might* be responsible. I see blood on my hands, that's it. But I didn't mean to! I *swear* I didn't."

"Yeah, I believe you," Bryar said. "Want me to try?"

"Yes, I do," Liza said. "Can you look, please? Maybe I'm blocked but you're not. Maybe I'm too close to it, you know? You *know* I don't do revenge spells on people. You *know* I don't go that far. Those things scare the crap out of me."

"Yeah, well, you should do them..." Bryar griped as an image of Mode flashed before both their eyes.

"Everything you send out comes back to you," Liza recited something Nana Bud had always told them.

But she was also on her sister's side. It *did* feel like Mode was getting off easy. He got the house she'd loved, the pretty little rock and roll opera wife, the few friends they had together, the money...Liza wasn't even asking for alimony.

"What about that woman with the Pizza Hut? Aren't you afraid you'll get back whatever you helped *her* do?" Bryar teased her.

Liza chuckled. "Not exactly. She didn't, er, walk away with what she thought she was leaving with."

"Yeah? You screw with her a little?" Liza could hear the excitement in Bryar's voice.

Liza snorted. She *had* screwed with Lola Ellen Pearson a little and didn't even feel guilty about it. "The spell I gave her cleaned up any issues they might have seriously been having in the kitchen, just in case, and then wiped the whole episode from her memory. Now, when she thinks of eating her rehearsal dinner there, she'll only remember the good parts."

"There are 'good parts' to having your wedding rehearsal dinner at the Pizza Hut?" Bryar sniffed.

"Yeah," Liza said, dropping down to her settee and kicking off her shoes. She didn't care if anyone walked in or not. "She told me she'd won eleven stuffed animals from the claw machine and her fiancé had played Alan Jackson for her three times on the jukebox. Said before the vomiting and diarrhea hit her; it was the best night of her life."

***

Liza blasted Christmas music all the way home, tunes from a station that played nothing but holiday tunes from country music singers. She sang along with the standards and hummed with the originals from people she didn't know, like Clint Black and Randy Travis.

"I can't believe you don't know who Randy Travis is," Colt had admonished her when he'd given her the ride home. "You know Eric Church but not *Randy Travis*?"

"I'm a new convert," she explained, a little defensive. "Okay, I admit it, it was a revenge thing. My mother hates country, says it reminds her of here. And then I was trying to find something that was completely different from the yuppie stuff my husband likes. You know, just to irritate him. He manages this pop opera group and even though I like them well enough I wanted something of my own. And then I found out I liked this. Joke was kind of on me."

"Joke's on you, all right. You're in need of a real country education lady," he'd drawled.

She was kind of hoping he'd give it to her. Someday. Maybe soon. She sure was thinking of him a lot lately.

In fact, on one lonely night when she hadn't been able to sleep she'd even thought of doing a little charm, just something to turn his eye to her.

But that would've been wrong. If it *had* worked, and it would have worked because she was *good* at what she did, then one day it would've backfired. He would've felt beholden to her and not known why and ended up resenting her.

Nope. She was going to get her divorce, wait a respectable amount of time, and then do it the old fashioned way...

With little dresses, cute shoes, a new haircut, and shaved legs.

Since it was already dark and the temperature said it was below freezing, Liza was surprised to see Jessie, her neighbor, walking along the side of the narrow country road.

She'd have *never* stopped and picked someone up where she used to live but it was different here and she knew Jessie. Sort of. Once someone had seen you move things around the room without touching them, you kind of developed a special bond.

"Hey!" Liza shouted above her Christmas music, slowing down beside the woman who was bundled in a puffer coat and long scarf. "You need a ride?"

Jessie hesitated at first but the lure of the heat coming from the window must have changed her mind because seconds later she hopped in and thanked Liza gratefully. "I was just up the road, visiting my mama," Jessie explained as Liza turned the volume down. Some Garth Brooks Christmas song about a bird and a girl named Maria.

"Everything okay?" Liza asked, although it was clear that everything was *not* okay.

Jessie grew quiet and gazed out the window. The sadness stemming from her was almost tangible and Liza felt it as keenly as if it were her own. She had a bit of her sister's sense of strong empathy herself. Liza decided not to press the issue hard, but tried to find a way to bring it up so as she passed her own driveway and headed towards Jessie's farm she said lightly, "I've had a rough week myself. I was accused of murdering a dude."

"Yeah, I heard about yours," Jessie admitted with a small smile. "Did you do it?"

"I don't think so," Liza laughed. "But that's going to be hard to explain."

Jessie shook her head. "I'm real sorry about that. Anything I can do?"

"I don't think so. I'll be okay."

And then Jessie began to talk. "It's my husband. The factory laid him off, right here at Christmas too. I don't know what we'll do. We got three kids and hadn't done no shopping yet. I *could* work, but we can't afford no daycare. He can get a job up in Lexington but the gas it would take to get there and back ever day would about be as much as he got paid."

"Geeze, I'm sorry Jessie," Liza replied, and she was. She knew that Jessie's husband worked hard and that they took care of her disabled parents and their three kids on top of that. Sometimes life just wasn't fair.

"I went down to the food bank today. They can give us stuff for Christmas dinner. But it's just so embarrassing, you know? And I filled out the Food Stamps forms? My husband's about to die he's so humiliated. We'll figure something out, but it's just stressful."

"Geeze," Liza replied. "I'm so sorry."

"Yeah, well, I don't want to lay all my problems on you or nothin'," Jessie said, shaking her head in frustration. "It just feels like if it's not one thing it's another. You know what I mean?"

"I know what you mean."

"We just try so *hard*. He works like a dog anyway and the kids ain't had new clothes in forever. I don't shop for myself, we don't go on no big vacations or nothing. It just don't seem fair," Jessie spat. "Just not fair."

Liza dropped the other young woman off at a small farm house encircled by towering pine trees. At the sight of their mother climbing out of Liza's truck, the three little faces that peered out from windows bordered with white flashing Christmas lights were nearly as bright as the bulbs.

Chapter Fifteen

ALTHOUGH SHE was in the treatment room, changing sheets on the bed; Liza knew it was Colt walking through the doors as soon as she heard the jingling of the bells.

After the week she'd had, Liza was happy to see a friendly face.

"Be out in a second!" she called, giving the corners one last tug. Her new sheets would be in within the next few days, but so far nobody had complained about the Walmart quality sets she had on her table.

"How's it goin?" he asked as she walked out into the main room. With his boots caked with mud and sap all over his brown coat, he kept a respectful distance and stayed on her "Welcome" doormat, not wanting to track in anything.

She did love a man with manners.

"Well, let's see," Liza began. "My business was trashed, the police laughed off my story, and then the guy I accused of trashing it wound up dead the day after I yelled at him in front of half the town at a BP station. So I've had better weeks. How about yours?"

Colt tried to smuggle a laugh but failed. The rich, vibrant sound rang through the room like music and unloosened a knot in her tummy she didn't know she had.

"Well, someone stole some trees from me. Just came up in the middle night and took some of my finest Douglas Firs. I don't grow them; I bring them in from the Carolinas. So that kind of pissed me off. Threw in some of the swags Filly made, too. That really got her goat. She's madder than an old wet hen 'bout it."

"People suck," Liza decided. "Sorry about that."

"Yeah, well, I tried to tell myself that maybe their kids needed a tree and they couldn't afford one."

He looked so sincere that Liza decided right then and there that she needed to become more like the Bluevine.

"At any rate, I'm looking forward to dinner tonight," she said with a smile.

And she really, *really* was.

"Listen," he began, his face turning a slight shade of pink and his hands twisting in front of him. "I want to say something to you but I don't want you to take it the wrong way."

Great, Liza thought, *I am going to be dis-invited to dinner because I killed a townsperson. Probably an uncle or cousin or grandpa or something.*

"May as well go ahead and say it; I'm a big girl."

But inside she was frantically searching out his mind, trying to probe whatever he was thinking. She failed. He moved too quickly for her to keep up.

"Well," he drawled, removing the hat from his head and fiddling with it like it was the most fascinating thing in the world. "It's my sister, Bridle. She's sick. She's had the cancer of the, er, female parts for a little while now. Had a rough time of it. Got divorced in the middle of the worst of it. If you could do anything to make things easier for her..."

He stopped then and his face turned an ashy white.

"I mean, you'll have to meet her first of course. If when you meet her tonight. If you could decide then. And I swear that's not the reason I invited you," he said in a hurry, looking up at Liza. "I swear. I wanted you to come an awful lot. I just thought about this part last night."

Liza felt a pang of remorse for Colt's sister, someone he clearly loved. And as she closed her eyes she caught a momentary glimpse of Bridle now, a lithe blond wrapped up in a quilt on a front porch swing, rocking back and forth and watching the bluish mountains in the distance. Her cheeks were pale and sunken, dark shadows hollowing out under her eyes. Her hair was gone but, if anything, it made her beauty shine through even more.

"Colt, I don't know what you've heard, but I can't *do* things like that. I'm not that..."

("Good" was what she wanted to say, but it didn't feel like the right word.)

"I know, I figured," he said hurriedly, humiliation staining his handsome cheeks. "And I surely didn't want you to think I was using you because I'm not. I sure do like you a lot, Liza Jane. Probably more than I should, seeing as to how you're still married and all. But Bridle? She's staying with me and you'll meet her at dinner. I was just hoping that when you meet her, maybe there's something you could say or do. Even if it's just to ease her pain a little. It's—"

His voice dropped off then and he looked down at his feet, abashed at his forwardness. "It's the last thing I could think of."

"I'll do the best I can," Liza promised him. "I'll talk to her."

"And please, if you need *anything* else done to the business, I'm handy with a hammer and nail. I can do just about anything," he said.

Liza smiled. "I think the whole town came in and helped. God forbid anything else should happen. I don't think it will though, since..."

Neither one had to finish that sentence; they knew what she meant.

***

Liza was running late. She knew she couldn't go to Colt's house empty handed, not for her first dinner, but she highly doubted a bowl of Ramen noodles would be appropriate. And crackers and cheese, even on her grandmother's fine china, would've been tacky.

Not that the discount grocery story had much to offer in the form of pre-made gourmet meals or party dishes. She finally settled on a cheese ball, crackers, and a bottle of wine.

And then she worried that his family was religious or something and didn't drink so she went back and exchanged it for a bottle of sparkling apple cider. She didn't want to walk into a dry house with alcohol and have everyone think she was a drunk. She'd have to save the drinking for home.

At first, as Liza pushed her cart up and down the aisles she was concerned that people were watching her and whispering about her behind her back.

"Girlfriend, you are super paranoid," she told herself.

Then she convinced herself that they were just jealous of her long black wool skirt, heels, and soft red infinity scarf. She looked nice; it was okay for people to look at her. She could dig that.

But then she knew without a doubt that it wasn't her fashion sense drawing their stares and gossip.

When a heavyset man in khakis and a Polo shirt approached her and called her by name, everyone on that side of the store turned and looked at her.

"Miss Merriweather?" he asked hesitantly.

Eh, close enough, she figured.

"Yes?"

His face paled a little but then he remembered what he was there for and jumped right into his speech. "Hi, nice to meetcha. I'm Tommy McIntosh, high school basketball coach. I don't know what-all you know about our team, but we've had us some bad luck these past few seasons."

The people who gathered around, pretending not to listen, nodded their heads in agreement.

"We got ourselves our first game right after Christmas. It would be real nice, for the morale of the team and the whole town really, if we could win that game. Now, you don't have to do anything to hurt the other boys. We're not into that. You don't have to do what happened to Cotton..."

The rest of the crowd shook their heads vehemently. Liza dropped her head in defeat.

"We just want our boys to feel *good* again. You know, to boost their confidence."

"Well, I understand what you mean," Liza said slowly. "But I don't know much about basketball so it would be hard to–"

"Oh, just some good luck's all we need. Just a little luck," Tommy winked.

After he had walked off, Liza was left scratching her head. They weren't going to ride her out of town on a rail because they'd thought she killed Cotton Hashagen–they were using it as proof that she might be of use to the rest of them.

She'd have to think about that.

***

Colt's house looked like Santa's workshop, all wooden logs and glossy windows, and winding wooden decks, and puffs of smoke coming from the two chimneys.

If only there had been snow on the ground, it would've been perfect.

The house, concealed from the road by the long meandering driveway, was all but suspended at the top of a mountain, surrounded by trees of all shapes and sizes. From the porch, it had a gorgeous view of all the valleys below. Liza thought it looked like a doll's house. She could see the tree farm below, acres and acres of Christmas trees, all planted in straight little rows, just waiting to be decorated and loved.

Liza had barely knocked on the door when it was flung open by a pixie of a girl who immediately threw her arms around Liza and kept hold of her in a vise, so tight Liza lost her breath. "It's so nice to meet you Liza!" she squealed.

Liza's muffled reply was something comparable in her captor's shoulder before she slowly detangled herself. "You must be Filly," she said at last.

"You ARE a witch!" she squealed again, clapping her hands together.

"Um, Colt showed me your picture, and I've seen the others so..."

Filly, undeterred, grabbed Liza by the arm and dragged her inside where the rest of the family waited in the living room.

Enamored of the stunning woodwork at once, Liza couldn't stop staring. With the exposed beams, elaborately carved mantle over a roaring fire, polished hardwood floors, exquisite crown molding–Liza could have looked for hours.

"My son did all of that," Whinny's voice came from the other side of the room. "Took him years. Did most of it himself."

Colt was nowhere in sight.

"It's a gorgeous place," Liza replied in appreciation, "But is Christmas tree farming really so...?"

"It's not from the trees," came a quiet voice from behind her.

Liza turned and saw the one sister she'd yet to meet yet, Bridle.

The beautiful, red silk Christmas scarf adorned with tiny candy canes wrapped snuggly around her head did little to hide the pale face and hollows under her eyes. She was thin, so thin that her bones in her cheeks and jawline were pronounced so that the skin stretched across them resembled tissue paper. Liza could see the tiny broken blood vessels and the purplish blood pumping below.

Still, she was beautiful.

Her eyes might have held shadows and bruises, but they were wide and alive, and she still held her full, pink lips and thick lashes.

"The tree farm is his passion," Bridle explained in a soft, brittle voice as she weakly made her way with tottering baby steps to an overstuffed chair. Liza immediately held out her arm and the other woman accepted it with gratitude. When their eyes met, Liza looked deep into the other woman and saw such goodness and joy there that Liza thought she'd do just about anything to help her. Anything at all. She understood Colt's near panic in her store.

"It's his music that pays for most everything," Bridle said, once she'd settled into the chair, and Liza had wrapped a blanket over her bony knees.

"His music?" Liza asked in surprise.

"He's a songwriter," Filly piped up. "He writes all kinds of country music songs for big artists. You've probably heard of them." She then proceeded to rattle off some hits that even Mode and Mabel's husband Gene (who didn't know anyone outside of Patsy Cline) would've recognized.

Liza was shocked.

"But why is he not living in Nashville or someplace else? Someplace with a music industry?"

"He *was*," Mare replied as she entered the room with a plate of Liza's cheeseball and crackers, taken from Filly when Liza first entered the house. "He lived there for seven years. Moved back here when Dad died."

"And when I first got sick," Bridle added.

"Not my kind of town," Colt smiled.

Liza turned and saw him standing in the door. He wore a silly-looking apron with a big smiling snowman surrounded by snowflakes and silver glitter. Flour coated his arms all the way up to his rolled-up shirtsleeves. Some had managed to get on his nose. He had a big grin on his face, though, and Liza watched as every female in the room, including her, regarded him with adoration. Without hesitation, he walked over to Bridle, bent down, kissed her forehead, and then lovingly straightened her scarf.

"Y'all hungry? Because I am starving," he announced.

She didn't think any man had ever looked more attractive.

***

Liza didn't think she could eat another single bite. Lamb. She'd eaten lamb for the first time since she'd moved out on her own.

And then there had been pie. So. Much. Pie.

Liza thought she might burst.

Not one moment of awkwardness, either, had passed amongst them. Well, okay, maybe *one* moment. It had come when Filly had declared, "So we hear you killed Cotton Hashagen for destroying your business!"

Liza's mouth had been full of mashed potatoes at the moment, and she'd almost spit them across the table at Colt's mother.

Not a *great* impression.

But she'd managed to swallow before answering, "Not exactly. I don't know what happened to Cotton, but it wasn't me."

Whinny had shot her daughter a **look** at that moment and then Colt changed the subject.

There had been no other talk of magic.

Once they'd all helped clear the table, they'd gathered in the living room where Colt had brought out his guitar. He'd sang country songs from people she'd never heard of, songs like "I'm No Stranger to the Rain" and "On the Other Hand" which made her realize that, indeed, her country music education was sorely lacking.

Bridle had excused herself after that, claiming exhaustion, and her sisters had helped her up the stairs.

"Does she stay here sometimes?" Liza asked.

Whinny shot a look at her son and let Colt answer. "She lives here," he said at last. "I couldn't have her home by herself. She needed to be with someone, and I can take care of her. I have more space than Mama does now."

"It's true," Whinny laughed. "I blocked the upstairs off at home. Too cold in the winter and I can't afford the heating bill."

Before Liza left, she asked if she could peek in on Bridle, to whisper goodbye if nothing else.

"Sure," Filly answered. "Her lamp's still on. She's probably just watching TV."

Bridle, in an old-fashioned white cotton nightgown, was indeed watching TV when Liza arrived–some black and white 1950's show. Maybe "Donna Reed."

"Liza," she smiled thinly. "Sorry to leave the party so soon. I swear it wasn't your company. Or maybe it was. Maybe you bored the pants off of me once you admitted you didn't kill Cotton."

Liza laughed. "I was just on my way out and wanted to say goodbye," she said, not leaving the doorframe.

"It's okay; you can come in."

Liza entered the room and sat in the rocking chair by the bed. Someone had built a fire in the fireplace, and it was cozy sitting there with the television on low and the warmth of the room seeping into the bones.

"I don't always feel so poorly," Bridle explained. "I had chemo today. It takes a lot out of me. But today was my last go around. So maybe things will get better now."

The look of hopefulness on her face was so optimistic that Liza smiled back, touched. Maybe Bridle was right.

"Where were you before Colt brought you here?" she asked, knowing she was prying but unable to help herself.

"At home," Bridle said thinly. "With my husband. He stuck around for a while but then he couldn't take it. He couldn't watch me be sick. He had to do everything around the house, work *and* take care of me. It was too much. He couldn't take what I was. What I am."

Liza looked down at the pale woman, surrounded by love and warmth, and lightness. And she was jealous. "My husband couldn't take what I was either. So he cheated. And then he left me for good."

"Men are pricks," Bridle laughed before going into a coughing fit that made her forehead shiny with sweat.

Liza leaned over, placed her hand on Bridle's forehead, and murmured a few words. The coughing stopped, her face cooled, and her head fell softly to the side. Soon, her chest was rising and falling in a deep, peaceful sleep.

It wasn't much, but Liza could, at least, offer her rest.

Chapter Sixteen

LIZA DROPPED off her holiday open house flyer at the Chamber of Commerce and then walked back to her building, astonished at how cold it was. She'd been vastly unprepared for the bi-polar weather of Kentucky. Having lived in Massachusetts for so long, she was used to the cold and snow and figured that with Kentucky's obvious geographic location she'd be enjoying a much milder climate.

She was wrong.

That morning she'd woken up to an outside temperature of thirty-five degrees and, according to the weather forecast, it was meant to get colder over the next few days. When she'd visited over the summer, she'd all but melted in her rental car, driving around in the upper 90s.

Liza thought that dropping off her materials would just be a matter of paperwork, a small errand of little importance. She'd applied for her business license with little fanfare and didn't expect the handing over of a flyer to be any different.

But Effie Trilby had been in the office and had introduced Liza around to several other people who were there for whatever reason and then she'd been invited to stay for breakfast because someone had apparently decided just to wake up that morning and feed everyone in the office. Someone had led her to a table full of biscuits, gravy, bacon, what someone called "breakfast potatoes," and several jars of homemade jams and jellies.

When she'd left, one of the women had handed her a plate stacked with biscuits. "You need some meat on those bones," she'd told Liza. "Take those for later."

Everyone had been extraordinarily friendly and seemed to be genuinely excited about her business. They'd all had nice things to say about her grandparents and promised to stop in and visit her soon.

For at least a few minutes, Liza had felt like she was part of a *something*.

***

And then, just like that, her mood plummeted.

She was a wash-up. Her business was a failure. That was all there was to it. Two people had canceled–the only two appointments she'd had on the schedule. Then the damn detective had returned, questioning her about Cotton.

Word *had* to be all over town by now: She was a witch with real powers, and if you double-crossed her she'd hurt you or worse.

People thought she'd killed one of their own, and now they wanted nothing to do with her.

After not a single client had entered her business all day, Liza did the only thing she *could* do–she stopped by the grocery store, bought two gallons of Rocky Road ice cream, and went home and ate them both.

But then, once she was full and had cried a few dozen times and was starting to suffer a tummy ache, Liza realized she was going to have to go about it a different way.

People canceled appointments. It happened. It was all part of running a business.

People *would* believe bad things about her. That was bound to happen, too. She couldn't stop that from happening, either.

All she could do was take care of herself and do what she could.

All her collectible cola bottles began rattling in unison, threatening to fall off their shelf, and Liza jumped to her feet. She ran and knelt on the floor before them, trying to steady them before another crashed to the ground.

"Okay, okay. I get it; I get," she mumbled. "I get it."

And then someone knocked on the door.

Before Liza had even turned the knob all the way, Jessie from next door was flying through, sleet turning her coat to ice and dripping tiny puddles on Liza's floor. But Jessie's cheeks were flushed with excitement, rosy and happy.

"Guess what, guess what?" she sang, all but jumping up and down as the cold wind rushed past her and chilled the living room.

"Um, what?" Liza asked, trying to echo the woman's cheerfulness.

"He got a new job!" Jessie squealed. "But, even better than that, his uncle who died a year ago? Everything is out of probate. My husband got more than $6,000 left to him. We're going to have it by Christmas! Can you believe it?! We've been waiting forever!"

She gripped Liza in a frigid squeeze and before Liza could say a word of congratulations, Jessie was running back into the night towards her old Ford truck, oblivious to the cold and ice. She wasn't even wearing a coat.

Somewhere in Liza's house, a bell jingled fiercely.

Chapter Seventeen

LIZA WAS MORE of a night ritual kind of gal, kind of the way she preferred to do her drinking around midnight, but sometimes, when the morning light was just right, there was nothing like a spell first thing in the morning.

It was that kind of morning.

Liza could not cure cancer. As much as she would like to, she just couldn't. But she'd met Bridle, she'd heard about why her husband had left her, and she'd looked into her eyes.

She couldn't, in good conscious, not try something.

After giving Bryar a call and filling her in on her plans, she also knew she had some backup.

People in the music industry feared Bryar, not because she was also a witch (most didn't know) but because she was a bitch. But Liza knew her other side, the sensitive side–the side that would do just about anything for anyone.

So, five states apart, both women sat down at their altars and began the formalities for what needed doing.

Liza put everything she had into the spell. She chanted, she poured water, she mixed herbs, she sprinkled oil, she called to multiple deities, and by the time she was ready, she took in as much of Bridle's pain as she could. She took in as much until she was writhing on the ground, crying and screaming from the power of it.

And that was where Bryar stepped in, ready to soothe Liza's discomfort.

Hours later, she awoke. Her joints were stiff, her muscles were tight, and she had a migraine from hell, but her mind was clear. And, above all, there was a sense of peace surrounding her.

That was when she whipped out the scissors. Because, unfortunately for her vanity, there was one more part of the spell.

Liza had talked herself out of it, at least, half a dozen times, but, in the end, it didn't matter. She did it for Bridle and the awful husband of hers who couldn't hack it with a wife who had cancer.

She did it for herself and her awful husband who couldn't hack it because his wife was a witch and he'd always feel inferior, no matter how much she gave him.

The hair landed in red puddles at her feet, like blood. She was finished.

Both women had done what they could. Whatever other energy was out there would have to do the rest, along with Bridle's body.

Then, Liza did the last, and possibly most important, part of the ritual: She got on Amazon and ordered every fluffy bathrobe, beautiful cotton nightgown, and aromatherapy body wash and bubble bath she could find and had them shipped straight to Colt's house.

Sometimes, being pampered and getting gifts were the best possible treatments a lady could receive.

God bless the internet.

***

As Liza unlocked the door and walked inside, she was still feeling the afterglow of her experience with the spell she'd done that morning, even though she was as bald as a baby's bottom. And, as tired as she felt, she was starting to build excitement for the day ahead because she'd convinced herself it was going to be a *good* one.

So when her phone went off, singing Mode's special ringtone ("You're So Vain"), she almost didn't answer it. Why ruin a perfectly good morning?

But then she decided against it. Ignoring him wouldn't work. He'd either keep calling or would call her mother or sister, increasing the drama. Best to deal with him and get it over with.

"Were you still asleep?" Mode demanded after exchanging polite, forced pleasantries.

Liza began her morning shop duties of turning on lights, straightening up from the day before, and lighting candles while she talked. She'd created a routine for herself and wasn't going to deter from it just because he probably had a bug in his bonnet.

"No, I wasn't asleep. I was at work," she replied, trying not to sound annoyed.

"Oh yeah? So you're really doing that?"

Liza tried to make do with letting out a string of curses in her head.

"Yes, it's still going." *Moron.*

"Well, I'm glad to see you've found things to do down there. That will be good for you," Mode said smoothly. "At least you're not just sitting around."

Like I did when I was married to you? But she kept that to herself as well. In fact, she was doing such a good job of not screaming at him that she felt she deserved at least a few after-work martinis when she got home.

Heavy on the vodka.

For now, she tried a different tactic. "Definitely not sitting around. I had breakfast with friends this morning and tonight I'm having dinner with someone's family."

She didn't mention that the "friends" were her sister and Bridle's energy. What he didn't know would just help irritate him.

"Oh, I didn't know you still had old friends down there," Mode said.

"These are *new* friends. And the family actually belongs to a man I met during my first week here. He's been around quite a bit, and I just had dinner with them in fact."

She *might* have fudged a little there, too, since it wasn't like he'd really been around a lot, but whatever entity existed would surely forgive that tiny white lie.

"You've been seeing a man?" The idea seemed to upset Mode's groove and for a second his pitch rose and he sounded as flustered as he *could* sound.

"Believe it or not, you didn't turn me lesbian," she replied.

"And you don't think it's–"

"Please don't tell me that 'too soon' was going to be at the end of that sentence," Liza laughed.

She returned to her counter to retrieve the matches for the candles, feeling pretty good that he wasn't getting to her that morning. She was in a good mood. She even felt that Nana Bud's snowflake silk scarf looked fetching on her head.

"You won't sign the papers, but you're going on a date. That makes a lot of sense Liza."

And, just like that, her good mood vanished.

Temporarily giving up on her morning routine Liza slumped into the nearest chair and frowned. "What?"

"You've had the divorce papers for weeks, Liza. I know you signed *for* them. Why haven't you *signed* them?"

Liza didn't know how to respond because she didn't know *why* she hadn't signed them. They were on the dining room table, had been there since the day after she moved into the farm house. She'd taken the pen to the table and then got distracted by a phone call. When she'd returned to sign them later, she'd suddenly had the need to go to the bathroom.

And so it continued.

She thought about those papers every day. They called to her from the dining room each time she walked by it.

But she just couldn't do it.

"Is it more money?" Mode demanded. "Is it something else you want from me? Are you trying to punish me? Is–"

"I don't know," Liza answered quietly. "I *don't* know."

She hung up on him gently then, not hearing the words he continued to say. When the room was quiet again, she spun around in her chair and studied all her shelves, the products, and the furnishings. She was making something good there; she knew she was.

So what was wrong with her?

Feeling a little less motivation than she'd felt moments before, Liza raised both arms high in the air, snapped her fingers, and watched all the candles come to life at once, their little flames sending dancing shadows all over the walls.

***

As much of an asshole as Mode might have been, he had a point. She hadn't signed the divorce papers. It was stupid, and she was crazy for not doing it. Something was obviously wrong with her.

But that wasn't the only thing.

She could *not* let people continue to think she killed Cotton. But she'd tried to see it herself and couldn't. If *she* didn't know then who did?

Liza was blocked by her own fears and confusion so a spell wouldn't work. And because she was blocked, Bryar was, too. There was only one thing left to do–visit the scene of the crime.

Her last and only appointment was at noon so as soon as Lola Ellen Pearson (ecstatic with the way her Pizza Hut "hex" had turned out) left, Liza locked up, buttoned up, covered her newly bald head with a wool cap, and headed out of town. She was going to find where Cotton died and go from there.

Maybe she'd pick something up. Hopefully, nobody would pick *her* up.

"I saw the blood," she said aloud as she drove along the mountainous road. "I saw myself with all the blood. So I had to be involved. I *had* to be. But I don't feel like I was..."

Since she couldn't drive all the way to the exact spot where his body was discovered, she had to park on the side of the road, cross the railroad tracks, and hike about a quarter of a mile.

The ice had melted from the leaves, making them wet and slippery. She tripped more than once, landing on all fours in the mud and debris. With a wet coat and wet pants and mud seeping through her knitted gloves, she was starting to freeze and think her adventure useless until she reached the area with the bright yellow police tape.

"Huh," Liza murmured as she walked around the rectangular shape. She felt a little thrill of excitement, in spite of the situation. It was like being on *CSI*. "So this is where they found him."

Well, she knew without a doubt that she'd never been there before. Although she wasn't afraid of the dark, there was no way she'd have been out there by herself, in a place she didn't know, trying to kill a man.

So what had happened?

Her vision had showed blood on her hands. But did that mean she'd actually killed him, or just had a hand in killing him? Was she guilty without actually being responsible?

Possibly.

"Well. Shit," Liza cursed, stomping her mud-covered Uggs.

There was nothing left of the crime scene, other than the disturbed bed of leaves and a slight hole in the ground, presumably from where he had fallen.

Liza knelt by the tape and closed her eyes. She could see him then, see Cotton. He wasn't running towards the location, but stumbling. His bulk had him heaving, unable to travel quickly. As he moved, he weaved, like perhaps he was intoxicated (although toxicology had found nothing more than Benadryl in his system). He held his head in his meaty hand, grimacing as though in awful pain. His face was red and contorted, but there was confusion there as well, and as he neared the sectioned-off spot, he stopped, looked up at the moon, howled a little like a coyote, and then plunged to the ground.

"Shit," she said again, because sometimes when all other words failed, the bad ones were still the best. "Shit, damn, fugger nut." (Because she could still feel Nana Bud's influence and energy around her and while her beloved grandmother might have cursed like a sailor, she hated the "f word" with a passion and Liza just couldn't risk a tree branch dropping on her head. Not when she was having a good makeup day.)

So what happened then? A stroke? A heart attack? An embolism?

All of those would've shown up on any autopsy worth a damn. So what had happened? And why *here*?

Had she killed him and not known it?

Damn, Liza thought with a little bit of pride. *I'm better than I thought.*

Now, how was she going to afford an attorney and keep herself out of jail?

Chapter Eighteen

SHE WAS CLOSER to figuring out what had happened; she *knew* she was.

In her purse, tucked safely away in a plastic baggie and sealed tightly, she'd gathered several of the leaves from the spot where Cotton's body collapsed. She'd also dressed in a pure white linen gown (even with the heat fixed, thanks to Whistle, it was still too damn cold to go naked) and left off the scarf. She wore no shoes, no socks, and no makeup.

She was ready. She would put an *end* to this.

It if it was true, if she'd killed him, intentionally or not, then that would be the end of her spells. It would be clearly obvious that she couldn't control herself and was not to be trusted.

Liza was just about to carry the rest of her supplies upstairs when a pounding on the door stopped her in her tracks. Sighing in frustration, Liza put everything down on the bottom stair and shuffled to the front door, her bare feet cold against the hardwood floors. She yearned for her fluffy socks with the unicorns on them, but they seemed a little insensitive for the ritual she was about to perform, so she'd left them off.

She'd left the hot pink nail polish on, though. Her feet didn't have to be *ugly*, after all.

Colt stood on the other side, all smiles and arms full of a large wicker basket. "Presents from the family," he announced. "And me."

And then his smile fell flatter than a hoe cake at the sight of her head.

"Dear God," he cried. "What happened? I'd sue if I were you. You didn't go to Sunny & Shears did you? I went to high school with her. Wouldn't trust her with one of my trees."

Frustration forgotten, Liza leaned over and sniffed. "Is that banana nut bread?"

Colt nodded. "And muffins and cookies and I don't know what else. But don't change the damn subject. What the hell happened?"

"I can't tell you," Liza hedged awkwardly. She wasn't ready and slightly embarrassed to admit it had been for his sister. She didn't want him thinking she'd done it to win him over or something stupidly female.

Without an invitation, Colt shook his head in disbelief and sauntered into the house. He made his way to the kitchen where he placed the basket on the table and then turned to face Liza who had followed him. "Also, I've got to tell you; they are already shopping for you."

"Shopping?" she asked, more than shocked. "For what? I have plenty of stuff."

"Not for a Christmas tree you don't," he chided her. "Filly has already picked out the tree on my farm, which I am meant to be chopping down tomorrow, and the rest of the girls are busy in town picking out ornaments. It's going to be a hodgepodge of mermaids, fairies, and unicorn stuff. I don't know what all they're cooking up. I didn't have a part of that. I even left Bridle propped up in front of the fire, knitting a tree skirt. She looked damn near chipper. Damndest thing I've ever seen. Just be forewarned."

"But why?" she asked, flabbergasted.

Although Liza *was* starting to feel a little sad that she didn't have any decorations up. Driving down Main Street had revealed that she was apparently the only person in town who didn't have anything out. And some people had gone all out, no matter what kind of condition the house was in.

Liza had actually seen one house with broken windows, a sagging porch, and garbage spilled out in the front yard, but there were lights thrown over everything that couldn't move and am illuminated Santa nailed to the roof.

And then there was the house with the tree carved to look like a penis. Well, it was *meant* to look like a morel mushroom but the two had striking similarities when it came right down to it. The homeowner had stuck an illuminated Rudolph on the tiptop of the mushroom head. Liza affectionately nicknamed it "the wee wee tree."

"Well, thanks. I appreciate it," Liza said sincerely, feeling touched and close to tears. Damn, she was getting sentimental. "I haven't decorated in a while. Mode wasn't home for Christmas much, and it just seemed sad to do it alone."

"Alone?" Colt snorted. "My whole fam damily will be over here to help you, hot chocolate and all. Only we do it Bluevine style—a shot of Baileys for a little kick."

"Sounds like my kind of cocoa."

He stood in front of her then, looking like a little boy with raindrops falling from his baseball cap. "But listen, I had another question for you. I was wondering if maybe you could come over and, um, just have dinner with me one night. Kind of like a date."

Liza froze, the divorce papers two rooms away calling to her: "Liza, you slut! Liza you ho! Liza you–"

Oh, shut up, she mentally snapped.

Instead, she reached out and touched his hand, cold and strong in her own smooth, warm one. "Colt, listen, I want to. I *really* do. I want to hear you play that guitar for me again. I want you to make me dinner because I like you and because I am hungry. I want to sit in front of your fire and curl into your chair and..."

"But you won't will you?"

"I can't," she said sadly, letting his hand fall. "I just can't. Not yet. You don't know who I am, or *what* I am."

"I know what you are Liza," he said gently, touching her face with damp fingers that even with their chill warmed her. "You are a fine, sincere, funny woman. And you're even pretty with that ugly haircut."

"But there's something else," she said, smiling a little at his last comment.

"I know," he replied stubbornly. "And I *don't* care."

But Mode had said that as well. And he'd been wrong. Over time, he *had* cared. She knew it wasn't fair to compare Colt to Mode but she couldn't do that again. *She* needed to know what she was, who she was, of what she was capable.

She had to know those things before she let anyone else in.

"I need some time. I need to figure me out."

Colt nodded but looked hurt. He started towards the door and had his hand on the knob before he turned and looked at her again. "I had to do that, too, Liza Jane. I had to figure out what I was and where I needed to be. And I did. I belong here. And you do too. You'll see."

And then she was left alone—bare feet, bald head, banana nut bread, and all.

***

It was after midnight, and Liza couldn't sleep. Every dead person she'd ever lost had visited her in her dreams, giving her random pieces of advice and talking over one another so loudly and with such intensity that she'd finally had to wake up to make them all shut up.

Her great aunt Agnes had been particularly vocal and she'd never even met her.

"Oh for God's sake, cut it out," Liza'd hollered into her pillow. "I get it; I *get* it."

And she *did* get it. She knew what she had to do.

Again.

And *this* time, she'd do it right.

At 12:30 in the morning she slipped into fleece-lined jeans from LL Bean, threw on two layers of flannel shirts, and then buttoned up her black wool coat. Lastly, for luck, she stuck on one of Nana Bud's old white crocheted hats.

She looked like a homeless hipster, but at least she was warm.

A little blinking light on her phone signified a new voicemail. She knew it was from Detective Kroner but, for now, she ignored it. If she were right, she'd have news for him soon enough. Good news.

And then maybe he'd never bother her again. That would be great news.

The roads were treacherous, covered in black ice that had her sliding from one lane to the other. The county only had two snow plows. Once it finally *did* snow, they'd have their hands full. And *her* driveway would not be a priority.

She needed to make friends with some snow plow guys ASAP. But first things first. First she had to prove she wasn't a mind killer.

It didn't take long to reach the spot where she'd need to park to reach the location where Cotton's body was discovered. When she pulled over to the side of the road, however, she hit a patch of ice, and her tire went over the embankment into the ditch.

"Well, shit," she grumbled. Well, she'd worry about that in a minute. Nobody was looking. She'd fix it when she had to.

In the meantime, she had other things on her mind.

Using her flashlight, Liza braced herself against the howling wind and ice pellets and made her way to the police tape. She might have been a witch and in tune with nature but she was still scared to be out in the middle of the night by herself. It was creepy as hell and every dark shadow made her jump. As a kid, she'd been terrified of *The Wizard of Oz* and those darn flying monkeys and, to be honest, they still gave her the creeps.

It was all still there, the police tape that was. Nothing had been disturbed. But then she recalled the leaves she'd taken with her, the ones she'd slipped under her mattress back at home. She'd hoped they'd tell her something in her dreams.

And they, along with all her head relatives, had.

Now, Liza turned her back to the police tape and faced the direction of her car again. Rather than walk the path that would take her straight to it, however, she began to walk diagonally. The icy wind was at her back now and pushed her forward, freezing her to the bone. She didn't care. She was on a *mission*.

It didn't take long until the train tracks were in sight. A train was currently coming down the track about a hundred yards away, moving much faster than she'd anticipated. The noise was astounding and the wind it kicked up chilled her blood and bones. She'd never been that close to a moving train before, and it actually blew the hat off her head. Liza waited until it passed on by before retrieving the hat, now mud-covered, and pulling it back down over her ears.

Using her high-beam flashlight she scanned the ground near the tracks over and over again, looking for the things that could mean the difference between her reputation and jail time.

It took twenty minutes of stumbling over rocks and sticks and leaves, and she was just about to give up when she finally saw it.

There, poking through the wet leaves, was a steel-toed work boot. If one hadn't been looking for it intentionally, they might have missed it. Indeed, several people *had* probably walked right over it and either not seen it or not realized its significance.

"Ah ha!" Liza cried as she whipped out her digital camera. The flash nearly blinded her in the blackness of the night, but her excitement was overwhelming.

After taking several shots and being careful not to move the boot, she moved on a little bit further and trained her eyes and flashlight upwards.

She was right again.

There, hanging from a skeletal tree branch, was a pair of glasses. Although the lens was missing from one side, they still caught the glare of Liza's flashlight and nearly blinded her.

Feeling vindicated, and not caring about the late hour, she first made a call to Colt.

"Stay right where you are," he warned her. "I'll be right there. Do not move."

And then she called the police.

***

Liza had promised Colt to stay put, but it was too damn cold. She wanted warmth; she wanted to wash her hands, and she wanted to be far away from the spot where a man had died.

So Liza headed to town, to her business.

She was singing to herself, feeling joy budding in her heart when she pulled into the parking spot in front of her building. She hadn't killed anyone. She hadn't been responsible for his death. It was an accident.

Liza heard the howling as soon as she neared her door.

At first, she thought it was the wind ripping down Main Street. The wind *was* fierce that night. She'd felt it all through her for hours.

But that was no wind crying for help. It was a woman, a woman in terrible pain.

Forgetting the key and using her own means of opening locked doors to get inside, Liza rushed in only to find her business in disarray again. Papers were tossed around, bottles of lotions broken, and a pillow on her settee had been slashed, the stuffing spilled out like snow.

"Damn it to *hell*!" Liza screamed, fury raging inside her.

But then she heard it again, that cry of agony.

Flipping on lights as she went, Liza headed straight to the treatment room. And there, lying on her massage table, was Athalie McClure. Athalie, waitress at the buffet. Athalie, the woman who had refused to take her drink order, instead sending someone else in her place. Athalie, the very pregnant woman Colt said he'd dated briefly in high school before he discovered her servicing two members of the football team behind the scoreboard at halftime.

And now, here she was, bleeding all over Liza's new sheets from Macy's. Destroying them again.

"*You* did it last time!" Liza cried. "It wasn't Cotton at all!"

"You're a witch! Your kind should be burnt. Your soul will burn in everlasting hell! You need to repent. You need to turn to Jesus and," Athalie momentarily forgot her sermon and let out a horrendous wail that would've shaken Satan himself.

"Oh for God's sake," Liza muttered, running to her stack of towels. She looked at her nice expensive ones and then shrugged and reached for the ratty ones instead. She wasn't *that* forgiving. "Have you called an ambulance yet?"

"No time," Athalie panted. "Oh my God, I am dying. God have mercy on my–"

"You're not dying, you're having a baby," Liza said as gently as she could.

Still, before she went to work on the wailing criminal before her, she called the hospital and ensured they were on their way.

The poor girl might have cost her thousands of dollars in damage, but at the moment she looked frightened and pained, and Liza couldn't feel anything but pity for her.

She also knew the ambulance wouldn't make it in time.

At first, Athalie resisted the words Liza chanted over her, the soothing touch she used on her trembling stomach and shaking legs. But then, as the pain decreased, she pleaded for more and between curses at the man who had done it to her she begged Liza for forgiveness.

And there, in her massage treatment room, Liza Jane Higginbotham delivered a tiny howling, little girl, the daughter of the woman who had ruined the best sheets she'd ever owned not once, but twice.

Liza figured that if the night ever ended and she ever made it home, she'd earned herself a bath of chocolate martinis.

***

"I guess we owe you a cup of coffee Miss Higginbotham," Detective Kroner said, the closest thing to an apology he could muster. "I mean, who would've thought it could a happened like that?"

"Well, *I* knew it wasn't me," Liza retorted.

The Bluevine girls had come over and decorated her tree, so at least part of her house looked festive. She was even thinking of stringing up some lights outside. But she'd wait until everyone was gone so that she could do that little bit of the work of herself.

Just for the fun of it.

"I've heard trains doing that to a person, hitting' them and knocking them plumb outta their shoes but..." Detective Kroner trailed off there and shook his head in disbelief.

"And Detective," a deputy piped in. "He *did* have that Benadryl in him from them bad allergies he had. Probably didn't even know what hit him."

"The coroner looked back over the autopsy. There was a large bruise inside his hairline, but it got overlooked because it didn't look like it was enough for a head injury," the Detective shook his head again. "Cotton always *did* like walking by the tracks at night when he had things on his mind. Liked to hear the night train. My guess is it knocked him into the woods, and he walked a little ways kinda stunned. Got lost maybe and then just dropped over dead."

Liza was sure that some people would still accuse her of being the one responsible for making him die in the first place, that she'd somehow made the train hit him. There would always be those who believed; always those who wanted to think badly of her.

But there was nothing she could do about that.

"And it was right kindly of you not to press charges on Athalie," the deputy added.

"She has a newborn. She won't sleep for a year," Liza laughed. "That's pretty good punishment."

But, the truth of the matter was, that baby (named Glory Nevaeh–or "Heaven" spelled backward) needed her mother. Liza wasn't going to stand in the way of that.

She was sentimental, too. She'd even sent a gift to the hospital.

Chapter Nineteen

"T AFFY" CORNFOOT was her first customer of the day and Taffy was as chipper as ever.

"Well, I know what all happened here to your business but I gotta say, you've done a better job than ever putting it back together. I don't think I've ever seen a prettier place. And right here in Kudzu Valley," she gushed while Liza rubbed on her shoulders.

"Thank you, and you know what the best part is? With the insurance money, I got to hire help!"

She could still hear Mare out front, ringing up the register and talking customers into things they didn't need. She was much better at that part than Liza had ever been.

"I'm just glad people are coming back around now that they know I didn't kill anyone," Liza said.

Taffy pushed Liza's hand away, sat up, and looked at her, barely keeping her modesty sheet covering her sagging breasts. "Oh honey, you think we don't know what you done here?"

"Huh?" Liza asked. "You mean people still think I killed Cotton, and they don't care?"

Taffy snorted. "Oh please. Jessie and her husband's new money? Well, that uncle of his drank everything away. No way he had an inheritance. And my legs haven't been swollen in a month. Not since you got here. Whistle getting that gig up in New York City as the replacement Santa at Macy's? There were hundreds of people in line for that. And poor little Bridle..."

Liza's cheeks flushed as she looked down at her heavy boots, a far cry from her high heels. Sometimes a girl *had* to make adjustments, no matter how painful they were. "I couldn't help Bridle."

"Please," Taffy grunted, a very unladylike sound. A large rosy nipple slipped out, and she didn't even bother to cover it up. Liza looked away for the sake of modesty. "We *know* about the rest. That was a different kind of magic. Her cancer's in remission, that's for sure, but it was pure old fashioned friendship that helped her. The little gifts? The calls? The visit you done when nobody else was there? And shaving yourself baldheaded to keep her company? That's magic not even a witch can make–that's friendship. The best *kind* of magic."

Taffy, finished with her speech, flopped back down on the table. "Now rub, girlfriend, rub the tar out of me. I got four ex-husbands got me stressed. Beat 'em out."

***

From toddlers to the elderly in wheelchairs, the whole town was gathered out in the streets when Liza left, all waiting to see the lights turned on up and down Main Street. Carolers stood on the front porch of the courthouse, singing Christmas songs out of tune and out of synch while elementary school children clogged on the sidewalks, a complicated routine that made it looked like their feet were on fire. Some looked like they were really into it; some looked bored, but all knew their steps.

Dozens of parents knelt before them, tablets and digital cameras videotaping and flashing lights to preserve their little darlings for years to come. Soon, their images and videos would be smeared across social media.

Liza stood and watched, her heart full of love for her new place. Someone walked by rolling a little cart, selling glow-in-the-dark bracelets and inflatable SpongeBob balloons. There was a food stand by the steps, eight people deep waiting, and the scent of sweet kettle corn drifted over to Liza's door and made her mouth water.

It would take a while to get used to the inconveniences.

To not be able to run to a big chain grocery store and buy organic fruit and veggies when she wanted, that could be a problem. To watch a newly released movie at the cinema on a whim, to go with her girlfriends to a bar, or go to a bar in town at all...those were sometimes hard to take.

But it was going to be *home*. After locking the door behind her, Liza walked over to the mailbox on the sidewalk, opened it, and closed her eyes. The thick envelope slid down the chute and landed with a "thump."

Liza said a silent goodbye to the last vestige of her marriage. It was over for good. The papers were signed. She never had to see Mode or hear from him again.

The feeling was bittersweet. She'd loved him once.

The singing stopped when she reached the end of the sidewalk but then an audible groan went up through the crowd. Someone had apparently flipped on the lights, but the town remained dark.

The lights, all the lights the volunteer fire department had strung up and down Main Street and Broadway were out.

Somewhere, a small child began to sniffle and then another one wailed. Even the older folks flashed looks of disappointment between each other.

With a smile and a wink, Liza raised her hand, waved it around once, recited words that were second nature to her, and the entire town suddenly transformed into a magical winter wonderland.

A small boy, maybe six years old, looked up at her and gasped. Liza gazed down at him, winked, and began to walk away.

***

Bridle, looking much healthier with her glowing cheeks and bright smile, was almost animated. She sat on Colt's front porch, wrapped snuggly in a colorful patchwork blanket, enjoying the night sky from the handmade rocking chair when Liza approached the top of the driveway in her truck.

Someone, Colt she'd imagined, had wrapped all the pillars on the porch with white twinkling Christmas lights and had hung a beautiful wreath on the front door. Candles were burning in all the windows, upstairs and down, and an inflatable Santa Claus was filling his sleigh with the help of the elves in the front yard. Animated deer, strung with lights, filled the yard and Liza laughed as she watched them move their heads up and down.

It looked like a fairyland and she knew he'd done it for his sister. And maybe even for himself. He loved Christmas as well.

"I decided to enjoy being outside for a while," Bridle explained, as Liza neared.

Her voice was still brittle but stronger than it had been the last time Liza'd seen her. A new light burned in her eyes that had nothing to do with the tiny bulbs surrounding her.

"I don't blame you," Liza agreed, settling on the stairs by Bridle's feet. "It's beautiful here. The sky looks bigger somehow."

Bridle nodded. "Colt always knew he'd build his house here. He said he felt close to the gods here. I think he's right."

Liza said so as well.

"Thanks for the visits and the little gifts," Bridle said shyly. "I love the bathrobe. I live in it, which is why it's being washed. It was starting to stink."

"I bought myself one after my husband left me," Liza admitted. "It got to smelling so bad I finally had to trash it. But they don't make any better."

"You know, you're the only one other than family who really came by and visited me through all this," Bridle confessed. "Thanks for that, too."

Liza didn't know what to say, so the two women sat in companionable silence. Until Bridle broke it again.

"Why won't you give my brother a chance?" she asked suddenly, never missing a beat with the rhythm of her feet as she rocked back and forth. To Liza, the rocking sounded like a song, a melody that was both foreign and familiar to her.

"It's complicated," Liza replied. "I was married once before, like you, and he...he was afraid of me I think. It made *me* afraid of me. I was afraid to do the things that I loved. And that made me someone else."

"Someone you didn't like?" Bridle prodded gently.

"Yes."

"It was the same with me, but for different reasons."

"But Colt loves you, he wants to take care of you. It's different. You're family," Liza persisted, feeling beads of sweat gathering on her forehead despite the cold wind.

"Colt didn't care what I was going through. He loved me. He *loved* me," she repeated vehemently. "He's not afraid of anything. Except for maybe Nashville. But that's another story. He hates the traffic and not being able to get biscuits the way he likes them. He's not afraid of *you*, either. I can promise you that. You won't have to change for him."

"But I thought that before and–"

"Colt isn't like that. He doesn't care what you do, or who you are. He can see through those things," Bridle argued.

"Maybe," Liza answered, but she didn't quite believe it. Mode had thought he could handle it. And he couldn't.

"Let me ask you something else...Everything you do is for someone else. And they're all little things. Jessie, Taffy, Athalie, me...isn't there something you could do for yourself?"

Liza giggled. "I straightened my front porch. And I fixed some things in my business when they got destroyed. But let's keep that on the down low and make the construction guys feel good about it."

Bridle waved her thin, delicate hand in the air. "Those don't count. They're practical and boring. Be *you*, Liza. Do something for *you*. Something that will make you feel better. Something that will make you feel happy and powerful and wonderful. Isn't it time to accept you? To make yourself happy? To honor your gift? And not by opening a business or selling stuff or moving but by honoring your talents?"

Something snapped in Liza's heart then, as she thought of the things she loved, the things she'd missed, and the things she wanted.

Then, looking up at the dark sky, she laughed. With both arms high in the air, Liza rose to her feet and began twirling. She spun so quickly it seemed like it was the world around her moving as she stood stoic in the center.

And then, as dark and quiet as the sky had been, it was suddenly filled with the pure, white flakes of snow. Thick and soft they rapidly fell around her like flower petals, landing on her eyelids, shoulders, and on Nana Bud's crocheted hat.

Bridle, too, got to her feet and tottered off the porch, reaching for Liza for support. Both women locked fingers and looked up, reveling in the first snow of the season.

And then there was Colt.

Liza stopped smiling then when she saw his scowl. She paused, about to make it stop, when he broke out into laughter and reached for her, taking her into a waltz. "Looks like somebody beat you with a pretty stick," he said as Bridle settled down on the porch step and continued to gaze at the sky in wonder. "Guess this means I'm going to have to break out the sled now." But he didn't look unhappy.

"It's going to be a good Christmas," Bridle declared, watching the two of them.

Liza wrapped her arms around Colt's neck and nuzzled him close.

It *was*.

THE END

Let's Connect!

Pinterest: https://www.pinterest.com/rebeccapatrickh/

Website: www.rebeccaphoward.net

Email: rphwrites@gmail.com

Facebook: https://www.facebook.com/rebeccahowardwrites

Twitter: https://twitter.com/RPHWrites

Instagram: https://instagram.com/rphwrites/

Rebecca's Other Books

To see a complete list of Rebecca's books, and for ordering information (including signed paperbacks) visit her website at:

www.rebeccaphoward.net

Taryn's Camera Series

Windwood Farm (Book 1)

Griffith Tavern (Book 2)

Dark Hollow Road (Book 3)

Shaker Town (Book 4)

Jekyll Island (Book 5)

Black Raven Inn (Book 6) **Coming February 2016**

Taryn's Pictures: Photos from Taryn's Camera

Kentucky Witches

A Broom with a View (coming December '15)

Broommates (Coming March '16)

A Broom of One's Own (Coming June '16)

True Hauntings

Haunted Estill County

More Tales from Haunted Estill County

Haunted Estill County: The Children's Edition

Haunted Madison County

A Summer of Fear

The Maple House

Four Months of Terror

Two Weeks: A True Haunting

Three True Tales of Terror

Other Books

Coping with Grief: The Anti-Guide to Infant Loss

Three Minus Zero

Finding Henry: A Journey Into Eastern Europe

Estill County in Photos

Haunted: Ghost Children Stories From Beyond

Made in the USA
Middletown, DE
13 April 2024